EBURY PRESS

VAZHGA VAZHGA AND OTHER STORIES

Imayam is the pen name of V. Annamalai, a schoolteacher and a writer. He has published seven novels and six short story collections, and been honoured with several awards, including the Tamil Nadu State Award (2010), Iyal Lifetime Achievement Award (2018), the Sahitya Akademi Award (2020) and the Kuvempu Rashtriya Puruskar (2022).

Prabha Sridevan is a former judge of the Madras High Court (2000–10) and former chairman of the Intellectual Property Appellate Board (2011–13). She has translated several works from Tamil into English, including *Echoes of the Veena and Other Stories* (short stories of R. Chudamani), which won the translation award at the 2019 Valley of Words Literary Festival in Dehradun.

Celebrating 35 Years of
Penguin Random House India

VAZHGA VAZHGA

and other stories

IMAYAM

Translated from the Tamil by
PRABHA SRIDEVAN

EBURY
PRESS

An imprint of Penguin Random House

EBURY PRESS

USA | Canada | UK | Ireland | Australia
New Zealand | India | South Africa | China | Singapore

Ebury Press is part of the Penguin Random House group of companies
whose addresses can be found at global.penguinrandomhouse.com

Published by Penguin Random House India Pvt. Ltd
4th Floor, Capital Tower 1, MG Road,
Gurugram 122 002, Haryana, India

First published in Ebury Press by Penguin Random House India 2023

ISBN 9780143461869

Typeset in Sabon by Manipal Technologies Limited, Manipal
Printed at Gopsons Papers Pvt. Ltd., Noida

www.penguin.co.in

Vazhga Vazhga

1

'The child has been shivering with fever for the last two days, should you not take him to the hospital?' Andaal asked.

'Yes . . . we must.' When Valarmathi dragged her words in a non-committal way, Andaal got angry.

'Why are you mumbling?'

'Can I go to the hospital swinging empty hands?' When Valarmathi asked this, Andaal got even more angry.

'Just because you don't have the money, can you keep the sick child at home? Shouldn't you at least take him to the government hospital?'

'Yes, I'll do that.'

'Only if you go to a private clinic will they demand 500 and 1000, just for a tablet, this and that, no?'

'Yes, I'll do that.' Valarmathi went to the front door as if she did not want to discuss this matter any longer.

3

Andaal saw Valarmathi walking away. The child, lying near the *nel kuthir* where grain was stored, was shivering and moaning with fever. She lost her temper. She was also in tears.

'Why my daughter got married to a murderous wretched devil . . .' She cursed her son-in-law, Senthil Kumar. She placed her hand on the child's forehead. It was burning hot. The phlegm was blocking his breath . . . '*Grrr . . . grrr*'. He was struggling to breathe and his body was limp. The more she looked at him, the more her temper and tears increased. She thought she would ask Sornam in the next house or Kannagi in the opposite house to loan her some money. With that, Valarmathi could take the child to the hospital. She came out of the house.

2

Venkatesa Perumal was talking to Kannagi in the opposite house. He saw Andaal coming out.

'Where are you working today, Amma?'

'Wherever I'm called, I will go.'

'Will you come to the meeting?'

'What meeting?'

'Our leader is coming. She will be campaigning for elections. From our town, three vanloads of people are going to attend. Will you also come?

'My grandson has a fever. I am thinking of taking him to the hospital.'

'If you come, you will get Rs 500 and a sari.'

'I must go to the hospital,' she said and turned to go back. He came near her.

'Kannagi is coming, Sornam *periyamma* [aunt] is coming with her granddaughter and then Gomathi *anni* [sister-in-law] is coming. From our street, more than ten persons are coming.'

Andaal asked Kannagi, 'What? Are you also going to the meeting?'

'He is stubbornly insisting that I should. I am not able to say no. So, I think I'll go.'

Andaal was in a dilemma about whether to go to the meeting or not. Seeing her hesitate, Venkatesa Perumal urged, 'Are you coming or not, tell me. I must go and ask others.'

Andaal did not say anything. If she went, she would get money, if she got money, she could send Valarmathi to the hospital with the child. She knew this. At the same time, she was also worried about how long it would take for her to return if she went to the meeting. She stood there, undecided, thinking that she could decide after she knew who all in her street were going.

'Are you coming or not? If you want the money and the sari, come.'

'Where to?'

'Vriddhachalam.'

'When is the leader coming?'

'Ten in the morning.'

'When should we leave?'

'You change your sari and we can leave.'

'The meeting will only be in the night, no?'

'This is election time, isn't it? Our leader will address this meeting in the morning itself and then she will proceed to the next meeting.'

'At least if it is in the evening, I can think of coming. You say morning. Who will come in this heat and die?'

'Is the heat blazing for everyone or only for you, Amma?' Venkatesa Perumal jeered.

'When will we return?'

'They say it will be at 10 a.m. Even if it gets late, it will all be over by 10.30 or 11 a.m. It takes fifteen minutes to go to Vriddhachalam from here and fifteen minutes to come back. Right?' His phone rang and he answered it.

'Just five minutes. The van has come. We just have to get into it. Just wait a second. I'll be back.'

'When will you give the money?'

'It is usually given after the meeting is over.' He sounded angry.

Chellammal, who lived to the north of Andaal's house, heard all this and asked if she could also come.

'Not just you. You bring all the people in your house. Rs 500 per head.'

'Even for kids?' Chellammal wanted to know.

'Tell me how many persons and I'll give you the money now.' Then he turned to Andaal.

'How long to wait for just one person? Don't I have to load people in three vans? Two vans have gone to the other colony. I must also see what happened there.'

Just then, Gomathi came there carrying water.

'Anni, will you come for the meeting?' he asked her.

'You come home and ask your brother for permission.' She went away.

'You decide and tell me. I'll go to the others and ask them,' he told Andaal and started moving towards Chellammal's house.

'If you give me the money right now, I'll come.'

At this, he turned sharply and retorted, 'Do you think I'll deduct fifty or hundred and give you the balance after the meeting is over?'

'My grandson has a fever; I must give the money to my daughter to take him to the hospital.' Andaal told the truth but he did not believe her, and with annoyance, thrust the Rs 500 in her hands. With the money in her hands, Andaal asked him when she should be ready.

'Right now. The van is parked near Chelliamman temple.' His phone rang.

'We will leave in five minutes, come to the van.' He answered the phone.

He took Andaal with him to Chelliamman temple. He pulled out a party sari (the sari with the party flag colours) from the van parked near the temple and gave it to her. He gathered more than ten such party saris in his hands and began distributing them at Kannagi's house, Sornam's house and so on, one after another.

3

Whatever may be his popularity among the party people, not even one person in the town liked Venkatesa Perumal. Before he joined the party, his family could not even afford to rebuild the mud wall of their hut that had fallen during the rains. He did not own lands even the size of a dhoti. His father, Pavadairayan, and mother, Chellammal, would be going up and down street after street, right from the morning, hoping that someone would give them work. When he was not working, Venkatesa Perumal would be playing cards in front of the Chelliamman temple all the time. But once he became the party branch secretary, he started going everywhere for the party and also began to wear an ironed white dhoti and white shirt. It was after these changes that the townspeople began to dislike him. First, he bought a cycle, then a TVS 50, then a Hero Honda, and now he had even bought a Tata Sumo. He had built a two-storeyed house too. Even those people who had five or ten acres in the town did not wear ironed white shirts or dhoti. But Venkatesa Perumal wore only a laundered dhoti and shirt when he went about the town. People seethed with envy when they saw this, as though slaked lime had been rubbed into their eyes.

Sometimes, people who belonged to the opposite party or even people with no party affiliations teased him when he went to the tea stall or the Chelliamman temple to play cards.

'Your *thalaivi,* your leader, she treats everyone in her party worse than a dog. How can you be in that party?'

Though he knew they were deliberately needling him, he answered patiently. 'Even if she treated them like that, she gives them posts like MLA, MP and minister.'

'So, to get a post, you will even lick another's boots if asked to, is it?'

He ignored this barb and just said, 'Are you deliberately provoking a fight? All parties are the same in Tamil Nadu.'

When the opposite party's people said, 'But this is seen more in your party', he snubbed them and said, 'In our party, the same person will not hold the post for 20–30 years like other parties. Our leader will make an ordinary man a minister and she will bring him down in one day from being a minister to an ordinary man.

In my party, anyone can become a minister. Do you know it was our leader who destroyed dynasty rule?'

'All that you say is true. No minister in your party sleeps a wink at night because he is worried that he may lose his job at any time. He feels as if burning coal is heaped on his head.'

The response came like a slap from Venkatesa Perumal.

'They behave themselves only because they are kept under tight control. Otherwise, each minister would have plotted and sliced their district, and sold them off long ago.'

'So, you may also become a minister one day?' They tried to taunt him.

'If it is written on my head that I should become a minister, who can change that?' The taunt was met with a snub.

'You put up posters and cut-outs depicting her as Kanchi Kamakshi, Madurai Meenakshi, Samayapuram Mariamman, Velankanni Matha and even Mother Tamil, *thamizhthai*. Isn't it too much? Even you . . . do you think it is proper?'

'Will all those goddesses give you MP and MLA posts? Our leader gave us those posts, so we put up posters. What's your problem?' The man who asked would be silenced by this reply.

Even if any ordinary person criticized his party, the Tamizhaga Uzhaippalar Munnetra Kazhagam (TUMK), or the leader of that party, he would tear them apart. He would never let down his party or their leader.

If he eulogized his party and their leader once, he would trash the opposite parties a hundred times more. And that too, criticizing the main opposite party, the Ulaga Thamizhar Munnetra Kazhagam (UTMK) gave him special pleasure.

'It is the same people who demand that Rs 3 crores be deposited for an MLA seat and Rs 10 crores for an MP seat, who lecture about democracy. But our party is not like that. Whether it is an MP candidate or an MLA candidate, no one has to spend a single paisa. Everything will be taken care of by the party. What more does a party-man need? Do you know there is no party like ours in the whole of India?' He would list the achievements of TUMK.

'Our leader, our thalaivi, is unmatched in beauty, intelligence, taking quick decisions and tossing the party-men around. You can't point to anyone like her in India. A person may be a big shot in the party but she can topple him down. No one dares to question her . . . not even to stand next to her and speak. Do you know? My leader is a one-woman army.' Venkatesa Perumal would rattle on as if it were one of the wonders of the world.

'You speak so much. Tell us why you alone are branch secretary, union as well as district representative, holding all three positions yourself?'

'Tell me who has worked for the party like me in this town? Do you know, I am the only person who is true and loyal to the party? Let them also work like me. The fellows sleep at home, are unwilling to go to a meeting and are afraid it may cost a hundred rupees. What chance do they have of getting any post? If they sit stuck at home because their wives won't let them go to party meetings, will posts walk to them on their own?' He would throw a challenge.

But he wasn't in this attacking mode all the time. When he was in a good mood and had no urgent work to be done, he spoke about the party and its problems as well.

'Being a party member is like climbing a steep mountain. The panchayat secretary will be one kind of person, the district secretary another. To adjust to everyone is like drinking salty water or tending to an elephant and a horse at the same time. Our party is worse than others. The other party people will cite rules and defy not only the panchayat secretary or the district secretary but even the leader. Not in our party. Here, we are not even allowed to stand upright. Whatever we do, we must be flat on the floor. Join our palms together and bend. We cannot even breathe loudly. If anyone steps out of line, overnight the man will lose his post. The real truth about a party or a post is that one stands on top of the other's head and proclaims that he is the best.'

If anyone started a conversation with him, that was all. He would not end it in a hurry. You cannot say that he would stick to the subject he started. He would jump from one subject to another and keep stretching the conversation. His manner indicated he knew everything. He did not let anyone get a word in, and even if he did, he would not hear it. He looked thin like a bamboo but his appearance was deceptive—it had no connection to the way he carried himself. If he began to speak, words came pouring out like water through a sieve.

If someone said that all the facilities are given only to party people, he would appear to be angry and frustrated.

'Being in the party and holding a post is like lying with a *kattuviriyan,* a snake. Every party man is a *viriyan.* Managing the party and the people is like swallowing a burning lump of fire.'

'If you feel like this, why are you mustering the crowd for the meeting? Only to earn money, no?' He would boil with anger at this question.

'The stupid people of this town will say that I am earning crores and crores of rupees by taking crowds of people to the meeting. By the time you take these people and bring them back, blood will ooze out of your eyes. Do you know that? All you can see is that the party man is wearing a white shirt and going in a car. Do all the party people earn money? Or get an MP or MLA post? Only the one who is the district secretary or minister can earn money. Do these people who wag their tongues know what happens in a party? You all talk as you please. A person who starts a company invests huge amounts and only then starts it. It is after that he earns piles of money. That is how it is, in a party. That is what politics is about. But do these people talk like that about businessmen? They will only jabber on about the party and the party-men.'

He would emphasize that being in a party and at a party post was like laying a tar road in the hot summer.

4

Though the local townspeople asked Venkatesa Perumal a thousand questions and made a thousand complaints against him, if he had any problem, the whole town would rally around him. That is because, out of the five or six hundred houses in his town Chinna Kandiyankuppam, 90 per cent of them belonged to people from his caste. Not just in Chinna Kandiyankuppam, it was the same in Periya Kandiyankuppam and the surrounding places. Everywhere, his caste was the majority. Even in the opposite party, caste parties or film star fans associations, his caste people held the important posts and were the ones who made decisions. They wouldn't let people from other castes hold even an ordinary post, like ward secretary.

Even on election day, if there was some dispute, they would call both the party people and say, 'Don't you know he belongs to our caste? Do not go on fighting. For us, caste solidarity is more important than the party. If we fight amongst ourselves, what will the other castes think? They will get mileage out of this and climb higher. Can we be a cause for that ourselves?' And they would not let the problem get out of hand.

Though the townspeople were envious of Venkatesa Perumal, they did not betray him. It did not easily harm him even if they did so on rare occasions. Since it was only people of his caste in the other parties too, they took care of the matter. Secretly, he did all the cheap tricks needed to ensure he was not harmed. He was not only focused on his growth, but he also saw to it that no one overtook him.

In the last two or three elections that had concluded, unlike what used to happen usually, TUMK got fewer votes in Chinna Kandiyankuppam. The reason for that was only Venkatesa Perumal's growth. It was true that there was no one as strong as him in the opposite party either. Even those who had intended to vote for TUMK, at the sight of his crease-less white dhoti and shirt, changed their minds and cast their vote for the opposite party. Therefore, at every election, the TUMK gradually got less and less votes at Chinna Kandiyankuppam. After the results were announced each time, the panchayat secretary would ask, 'What is this, not even half the votes came to us in your town?' His reply was always, 'There was a wave against us this time. Just see at the next election. If you open the ballot box, it will be filled with only our votes. The secretary too would not make much of this matter because he too wanted at least one person of his caste in the party in that town.

The party which was opposite Venkatesa Perumal's party TUMK was only the UTMK. Right from the beginning, it was Dhanasekaran who had been its member and branch secretary. He and his family may be in the party and vote for it, but they could do nothing more than that. This was because his caste was not the dominant one. As far as Chinna Kandiyankuppam was concerned, be it TUMK, UTMK or the caste-based party Uzhaippali Vargam, only Venkatesa Perumal's caste people's hand held the upper hand.

5

Andaal returned home with the sari and the money and gave the money to Valarmathi.

'Are you going to the meeting?' Valarmathi asked, taking the money from her.

'Yes,' Andaal replied casually.

'It will be very crowded.'

'Let it be crowded.'

'It will be very hot.'

'Is it the first day that it has been hot?' She changed into the sari that was given to her.

'Who else is coming with you?'

'Everyone in the street.'

'If this child had not been sick, I would have come too. I too would have got Rs 500.'

'Forget about the money. Don't forget to go to the hospital.' She peeped out of the house to see if the other women had started. She could see Venkatesa Perumal standing in front of the third house from hers, chatting to Gomathi.

'How hot it is in the morning itself! Can't imagine how it will be at noon. Who wants to come and die in the unbearable heat?' Gomathi asked.

'You are going to be in the van while going and again when returning. Are you going to be toiling there? No. Just sitting. If you come, you will get a sari and Rs 500.' He did not stop with saying this and stuffed the sari and the money in Gomathi's hands. Then he went looking for the woman in the house next to that.

'He is a really smart operator,' Andaal said, seeing him going up and down to each house. Then she sat down in front of her house, deciding to go when the other women gathered.

Venkatesa Perumal was now sitting in front of Chellammal's house.

He knew who the gullible ones in the town and the ones were who needed money. He knew who he should take to the meeting, who he should not, who belonged to the opposite party and who belonged to no party. He addressed the women as anni, *athai* (aunt), *pappa* (child), periyamma or amma, talked ingratiatingly and loaded them in the van.

'It will take a whole day. I won't come.' If anyone told him this, his answer was, 'What are you saying, Periyamma? Nowadays even those who go to a relative's wedding come back in no time. This is a party meeting. I'll just show all your faces to the panchayat leader and district leader, and the next second, I will load you all in the van and pack you off.'

He gave an extra Rs 100–200 to those women who brought four or five women with them. Some women were eager to get this extra cash, so as soon as Venkatesa Perumal called them, they rushed to get other women to go with them to the meeting. There were two or three women in the village who always did this.

If he took two or three vanloads of people, he displayed them before the panchayat and district secretaries and said, 'My place is virtually our party fortress.' He would have taken only three vanloads of people, but he would proclaim it was four. Both the secretaries knew very well that he was lying, but they turned a blind eye. Even if the expenses were five hundred or thousand more, they did not say anything. All that was important for when the minister arrived was a good crowd.

Some people asked him bluntly, 'Aren't you ashamed to earn money by rounding up women to meetings after meetings and giving false accounts?' He was not perturbed at all.

'Only the people who shout "long live", cheering another, will succeed. The one who says "down down" will never succeed. In public life, there will be a thousand things. One person will say "long live". Another will say "down down". Hundreds will spit at you. We have to tolerate it all. That is politics. If you shrink with shame, you can't come to politics. If you stay away to avoid humiliation and shaming, how will anyone become an MLA or MP?' He laughed in reply.

6

Kannagi came out wearing the sari designed in party colours, the 'party sari'. Very soon, Sornam and her granddaughter came out. Gomathi came out too. All of them discussed who looked best in the party sari.

Venkatesa Perumal came with five or six women from the North Street.

'Come, come, it is getting late. Shall we go near the temple? Or shall I ask the van to be brought here?'

'Ask them to bring the van here,' Kannagi said. At once he made a call and summoned the van.

'Will you also give money on the voting day?' Andaal asked.

'Then what? Who will vote nowadays if they are not given money? In these times even the party-men expect to be given money.' He watched for the van to arrive.

'How much will you give for a vote this time?' Andaal asked eagerly.

'At the last MP election, we gave Rs 500 for one vote. This time it is the MLA election. It will surely be not less than Rs 1000 for one vote. We may even give 2000.'

'Whatever the amount is, you will only give us after taking half of it, right?' Kannagi needled Venkatesa Perumal. Instead of answering her, he changed the subject.

'The party sari suits Anni so well, super!' he said, laughing.

'When we voted last time, it was only me. Now my daughter is also with me. The money for two votes must be given to me,' Andaal said in a peremptory tone.

Venkatesa Perumal replied with a light smile, 'Periyamma, don't you get money from all the parties?'

'Is it only me? The whole town does it. Though they get money from both parties, the people cast only one vote, right? After sinning by taking the money, how can we not vote?'

'That is really being fair!' Venkatesa Perumal laughed aloud.

'We must get the entire money for all the votes in our house,' Sornam declared.

'If you don't get the money, won't you knock at the door and quarrel? Won't you argue and ask if your vote is an invalid one?'

'When you give the money, let them be good notes, don't give torn notes.' When Andaal said this, he could not help laughing.

'Sure, I will ask them to print fresh notes specially for you.'

'During the last election, they gave brass pot, stainless pot and all in the nearby town, why didn't you?'

'During the local election, didn't they give a nose ring in one gram gold?'

'Will they give in the coming elections too?'

'They will.'

'Promise?'

'You just vote for my party, overnight you'll find it delivered at your house, on its own—stuff like a silk sari, earrings, nose ring, brass pot and stainless-steel pot.' He sounded as if he was taking an oath in front of a temple.

The van arrived. He went quickly and opened the door.

'Get in, get in.' He made Andaal, Sornam, Gomathi, Gayatri, Kannagi and others get in one by one and then he climbed in too.

'Drive to East Street,' he told the driver. The women waiting there got in.

'Drive to South Street.' The three women standing there got in. The van then went to Chelliamman temple and stopped. More than ten women were waiting there. They got in.

'I'll now go to the men's van. You must follow behind us,' he told the driver and went to the van ahead.

That van started and the women's van followed next.

7

Thirty-four persons were packed in a van with a capacity of just fifteen. There was not even any standing room. The driver kept shouting, 'Catch hold of the bar, hold the bar tight.'

The young women and children paid no heed to him and shouted, 'Play music, come on, put on the music.'

When the music started, everyone shouted with joy.

The van left Chinna Kandiyankuppam, passed through Periya Kandiyankuppam and joined the main road going to Vriddhachalam. All the women in the van looked at both sides of the road and turned speechless. They saw that iron poles were planted every five feet on the road, on which the TUMK party flag was tied. Between each pole were strung party decorations. There were cut-outs and digital banners measuring

20 ft x 30 ft and 30 ft x 40 ft. On seeing them, the children, competing with each other, shouted, 'Look at that, look at that.'

Every digital banner and cut-out excited the children more. They did not listen to their elders asking them to be quiet.

After it entered Vriddhachalam, the van moved inch by inch. There were hundreds of vans, cars, buses and minivans going together as though in a convoy. The entire town was filled with flags, hanging decorations, digital banners and cut-outs. As they kept seeing all these around them, the excitement of the children and young women passed on to the older women also. They looked around on both sides without blinking their eyes. The driver kept warning the children who stretched their heads out of the windows.

Manalur, which was the meeting venue, was only 2 km away from Vriddhachalam but it took more than an hour to reach there. After they reached Manalur and got off the main road, it took more than half an hour to reach the meeting venue. When the van reached the place allotted for parking, Venkatesa Perumal got out of the men's van. He ran to the women's van and opened the door.

'Get down.' He let them get down one by one.

Each woman and child climbed down and gazed in wonder at the crowd. They felt as if they had been transported to another world when they saw the preparations.

'An unbelievable spectacle. Two eyes are not enough, you need 100,' Sornam said.

'You kept saying you won't come. Now do you see what this looks like?' Venkatesa Perumal asked Gomathi. 'You must be fortunate to be a part of this,' he said with a smile.

Gomathi nodded as if in agreement.

'Come right behind me. If you come slowly, you won't get a place to sit.' He hurried the women and children and herded them away.

They reached the women's enclosure.

'Grab a place and sit down at once. Don't get separated,' he shouted.

Without waiting for him, the women and children ran ahead and grabbed chairs. However much he tried, he could not seat the Chinna Kandiyankuppam women and children in one row. They could only be seated separately in two or three rows. Even then the two women from the East Street did not get chairs.

'Shouldn't you run and get your chairs?' He frowned at them. Then he went some ten or twenty rows behind and somehow got two chairs after a search and brought them over. By the time he adjusted the two chairs to fit among the already arranged chairs in the row and made those two women sit down, he was perspiring heavily.

'What a crowd!' Gomathi was wonderstruck.

'This is nothing. Just wait and see, more will pour in.' Venkatesa Perumal was puffed with pride.

'Look at that! The people are crowding in like swarms of eesal, the flying insects! Will there be seats for everyone?' Kannagi wondered.

'This is nothing. All the people in our district will gather, just see.'

Just then a local man came looking for him. At once Venkatesa Perumal walked towards him. As he walked away, he warned the women, 'Remain seated. I'll come back. Don't get scattered.'

No one paid heed to him—they didn't care where he went. That was because all their attention was on the decorated dais, the flags and hanging decorations tied around it, and the cut-outs and digital banners placed there. Looking at the massive crowd, all of them without exception were open-mouthed in amazement. Overcome with eagerness, the women stood up from their chairs along with the schoolchildren. Among all of them, the oldest were Sornam and Andaal. They too, like little kids, stood up and gaped at the crowd and the decorated dais.

'It really looks like a magic place.' The words slipped from Andaal on their own.

The place was about 400–500 acres, and it had been flattened and cleared of trees, plants and shrubs to make space separately for a men's enclosure, a women's enclosure and a parking lot for cars, vans, buses and lorries. They had separated each enclosure with fences made of casuarina poles that were as tall as a man. They had also made spaces for the leader of TUMK to alight from the helicopter and get into the car to drive to the dais and again for her to return to the helicopter after the meeting ended. Each of those spaces was fenced by casuarina poles. LED screens were placed here and there for people to see the leader speak from the dais. There were many loudspeakers too. When Andaal saw all the decorations encircling the vacant ground behind the men's and women's enclosures, she really thought that it was a wonder world. She saw the entry path for people who were coming to the meeting. She could see the crowd coming in thick clusters, growing minute by minute. She looked at the enclosures where the men were, and the women and the vehicles. It was packed everywhere—a never-before-seen crowd. The more she saw, the more Andaal's joy rose. She laughed like a child.

'Hey sami! Really a wonder!'

8

'The platform looks heavenly. How much would it have cost? Rs 10,000 maybe?'

Kannagi glared at Andaal as if she had asked an improper question.

'Just one ordinary cut-out here will cost more than 10,000. Calculate for yourself,' Kannagi sneered.

'Sooooo much?'

'Just the platform would have cost more than Rs 50 lakh.' Kannagi sounded as though she knew everything.

'Hey sami! That's a lot.' Andaal was open-mouthed with surprise.

'The platform is fully air-conditioned, so it may be more than that.'

'Would they have spent Rs 1 crore just for today?'

'What you say is nothing. If they have given Rs 500 per head, how much would just the crowd have cost?

Then the van, bus and other things. For how many miles have they tied festoons and put up cut-outs and banners? My estimate is Rs 50 or 100 crores,' Kannagi said. Andaal looked at her and wondered how she knew all this.

'Why are they dumping so much money as if it is just trash?'

'To reap it back in crores. Why else?' Kannagi said sarcastically, looking at the platform and the crowds. 'They dump crores of money and earn more than that. That is none of our business. We have just come for the payment they gave us, no?'

'Does only this party spend like this? Or are all the parties the same?' Andaal wanted to know.

'Every party dumps money like this at election after election.'

9

Andaal saw in front of her, two women fighting and tugging at the same chair. Both the women were wearing the TUMK-coloured sari and only their blouse was different. The woman wearing a green blouse was plump and had a wheatish complexion. The woman wearing a red blouse was tall and lean, and her teeth stuck out a bit. From what they spoke, Andaal deduced that the green blouse woman was from *Periya* (big) Vadavadi village, and the red blouse woman was from *Chinna* (small) Vadavadi village.

The two women were violently tugging the same chair towards themselves and appeared to Andaal like two bulls fighting and knocking against each other.

'In this whole area, couldn't you find any other place to sit? You are fighting for the chair I found,' the Periya Vadavadi woman asked.

'You did not find this chair. I came first. It is you who are fighting for my seat,' the Chinna Vadavadi woman retorted.

While they kept tugging at the chair, the Chinna Vadavadi woman's elbow poked the eye of a woman sitting behind. Immediately, she sprang up in anger.

'In the squabble between you two, why the hell are you poking me? Can't you see people who are sitting?'

The Chinna Vadavadi woman turned round. 'Where did I poke your face?' As if she was waiting for this moment, the Periya Vadavadi woman tugged at the chair with force. Once she had it in her hold, she placed it on the ground and sat on it.

When she knew she had lost control of the chair, the Chinna Vadavadi woman tried to push the Periya Vadavadi woman off the chair. Then she tried to push her with the chair but failed again. She again tried to pick up a quarrel with the other and pulled her hand.

'*Chee*, take your hand away. Who are you trying to grab?'

The Periya Vadavadi woman pushed the Chinna Vadavadi woman away.

'After grabbing the chair that I had, are you trying to knock me down? Just wait, I'll call my townspeople and teach you a lesson,' the Chinna Vadavadi woman warned and turning towards the east, shouted to someone, 'Hey, Aarthi, hey Aarthi!' But in the crowd's clamour, her voice went unheard.

'Will you get up now and vacate my chair? Otherwise, there will be hell to pay.' She was fuming.

'Do what you can.' The Periya Vadavadi woman settled herself more firmly in the chair.

'If you are capable of rousing this noise for something that belongs to another, I can't even imagine the dust you will raise if it is your own chair.' The Chinna Vadavadi woman made faces at the other.

'What . . . has this chair come from your father's house then?'

'No . . .'

'Then why this ruckus?'

'You are from Periya Vadavadi, aren't you?'

'Yes.'

'That is why your mouth is so big.' She extended her arms as wide as an elephant's mouth.

'Enough about my mouth. You first shut your drum-mouth.' She widened her arms to show a big drum.

'I'll shut mine after you shut yours.'

'What is it of mine that is lying open?' The Periya Vadavadi woman mocked.

'Everything.' The Chinna Vadavadi woman grimaced as though she had seen shit.

The Periya Vadavadi woman was now very angry.

'Can't find a chair to sit. Mouth is like this . . . and stinks,' she spat out.

'I can sit too.' The Chinna Vadavadi woman plonked herself on the Periya Vadavadi woman's lap.

'Whose lap are you sitting on? Are you my kith or kin?' The Periya Vadavadi woman pushed the other down angrily. The Chinna Vadavadi woman reached out for the other's hair and tugged it with force.

When both the women started fighting, seven or eight women who were seated in that row tried to pull them apart. There was much confusion and noise.

Two or three women pulled the Periya Vadavadi woman off and made her sit on that chair. Five or six women dragged the Chinna Vadavadi woman to the next row, asked a schoolgirl to get up from her chair and made her sit there. Though the two women were now sitting in different rows, they continued to abuse each other. Their jaws did not cease moving. Looking at them, Andaal was taken by surprise.

'Look at them, how they fight in such a short time!'

'If the whole world comes, how will there be seats for all?' Kannagi asked.

'Soon there will not be room even to stand, I think.'

'When these people fight so much for a chair that belongs to neither, why won't the ministers and MLAs come to blows with each other?'

Andaal did not respond to Kannagi. Instead, she turned to look behind when she heard the voices of two or three women quarrelling.

10

A fair, middle-aged woman was seated on the fourth chair to the east of the casuarina barricade that separated the men's enclosure and the women's, in the row that was two rows from Andaal's. Three women were standing in front of her, talking to her. It looked as if the standing women and the sitting woman were fighting. There were three vacant chairs next to the standing women. Andaal could not understand why they did not sit when chairs were available. She turned a little more so that she could see and hear what was happening.

'Don't you understand me? Get up and go. How can you sit alongside us?' one of the standing women who was stout and dark asked the one who was sitting.

'This is a public place. Is it your house?' was her casual answer.

'Try sitting in my house. There will be hell to pay,' the dark, stout one said rudely and fiercely looked at the others. 'Just because everyone has gathered, can you sit as you please in spite of your caste?' she continued.

'You people won't change even in this place where people from everywhere have gathered, is it?'

There was a short dark woman next to the stout one. It was her turn now.

'Behave yourself and leave this place. You'll regret it if you don't.'

'Where is an empty place for me to go? People are jostling each other with no standing room. Can't you see?'

'Sit wherever you can. What do we care?' the short one threatened. Then, as though granting a favour, she said, 'If you want, take the chair with you and go.'

'How does it bother you if I sit here?'

'Everyone in this row are our street people. You alone are the outsider. Go . . . go.' This was the short one.

'I refuse to go. You show me a vacant seat, then I will go.'

'I'm warning you if you don't go now . . .' This was the stout one's stern warning.

'Are you trying to create a caste quarrel?' The seated woman was now angry.

'You are the one who is creating trouble by sitting in our midst.' This was the tall woman standing near the short one, who now said, 'If you don't get up now, we will ask our street men to come and pull you out and fling you away.'

'Try doing that, let us see,' the seated one said calmly, without getting provoked. Then she looked around as if searching for someone, to the front and back and on both sides. Her face changed.

'Will you get up or not?' the stout one asked. The seated one looked casually around as if the question had nothing to do with her.

'Get up now.'

'Who are you to ask me to get up?'

'What caste are you? And what caste are we? How do you dare to come and sit with us? Have you no brains?'

'This is a party meeting. Anyone can sit anywhere. I am the one who ran and caught this seat. You know that?'

'So what? Leave now.'

'I won't. Try what you can,' the seated one retorted insolently.

'Your tongue wags too much.'

'Did you feed and nurture it?'

'If you keep talking back without leaving, you'll get a bloody nose.'

'Let us see who gets the bloody nose,' the seated woman threw a challenge.

'Go bring our men, men from our place,' the tall woman told the stout one.

'Go bring anyone you please. Let us see what they can do. I'm just sitting in my chair. What else have I done? Did I come and try to socialize with you?'

This incensed the stout woman very much. 'Try it . . . come to my house and pick a bride for your family. Look at *this* thing . . . such impertinence.'

'Say anything you want. But if you dare to say that thing and this thing, you'll get thrashed. I have the same thing that you have, nothing different.'

'Only now all these wretches behave like this. It was not like this before and all,' the tall woman said.

'Are you going to get up now or what?' the stout one asked in a gruff voice.

'I won't.' She sounded authoritative.

'If you don't, your respect will go away in shreds.'

'How . . . by ship or plane? Let me see.' The seated woman was not cowed.

'Not going . . . and answering word for word, are you? Not just your mouth . . . your other thing will get stitched,' the stout woman said.

'Oh, you will, will you? And I'll quietly show it to you?' Then she went on. 'It was your street man who brought me in the van with the others. Call him if you want. Let him decide. You need me for the crowd, you need me to vote, but you won't give me a chair. What kind of justice is this?' As she was speaking, the stout one suddenly pushed her down and quickly occupied the chair.

Before the woman who was pushed down could realize what had happened, the tall woman quickly stacked the empty chairs on top of each other and sat on them to prevent the other woman from taking another chair. The short one resumed her seat in her chair. The woman who was pushed down was angry that not only had the other three pushed her down, but they had also made her chair-less and she glared at them.

'You have pushed me down and taken my chair, no? Just wait,' she screamed in rage and with tears in her eyes, she hastily called someone on the phone. She called again and again, but there was no reply. The tears welled more.

'You did not even care that I am from the same town as you and you pushed me down. I will make you pay for this.'

'You are not from our town. You are from the paratheru, the street where Dalits live.'

'I too belong to Pavazhangudi.'

'You may be from Pavazhangudi, but you come from paratheru and not from the town.'

'Then what is Pavazhangudi?'

'The town.'

'Then . . . me?'

'You are from Pavazhangudi but not the town, you are from paratheru. The two are not the same. They are different.' The answer was clear and categorical.

'Is that so?' she asked sarcastically and called someone on the phone.

The tall woman called a girl who was standing near the casuarina barrier and made her sit on one of the chairs that she had stacked and had now placed separately.

Andaal was looking at all this drama among the Pavazhangudi women with great interest.

'Look at this *koothu*.' She pointed the spectacle to Sornam, who turned back.

'You have pushed me from the chair and now I have no place to sit. I'll go right now and call my street men and teach you a lesson. Am I the only one who came here for the cash? These bitches also gathered here for the cash. In this, where does caste come from? All the bastards only do caste politics, who does party work?' she went away yelling.

'Why is this woman shouting like this?' Sornam asked.

'I think she is from the *colony,* that is why the quarrel.'

'Did she sit along with other caste women?'

'Looks like it.'

'Same town?'

'Sounded like that.'

'Why couldn't she have sat away from them? Even on the bus, these creatures do the same thing, standing shoulder to shoulder. These arrogant bitches.'

'Looks like they think castes will vanish when they come to meetings.' Andaal grimaced.

'All these dogs think like that.' Sornam turned her face away.

11

Young women were dancing to film songs on the stage and they began to show it on the LED screens.

More than ten dancers were there, dancing as though they were competing to find out who won and who lost. All the dancers were wearing identical costumes studded with shiny mirrorwork and they had all plaited and decorated their hair in the same style. Not one of them was over twenty years old. It was impossible to single out even one of them as tall, fat, short or dark, nor point out that one of them danced excellently or one of them did not. It was pleasant to watch them as they kept on dancing to song after song without tiring.

'Where did they learn to dance like this?' Andaal asked Kannagi in surprise.

'This is their livelihood.'

'Dancing . . . livelihood?'

'Yes.'

'Lifting the legs like this?'

'Yes.'

'Their bodies are shining with jewels that look like gold and not one of them is even a bit dark or wheatish colour.'

'If you wear powder and glitter, you will also shine like them.' Kannagi laughed.

'Your tongue wags too much. I'll tell your husband to clip it short.'

'It is daytime and even now they light up the stage with multicoloured lights. That is why every girl shines like this.'

'I love to look at their faces more and more.'

'If you yourself feel like this, just imagine how it will be for these male dogs,' Kannagi turned to Andaal and laughed. Then she muttered to herself, 'After looking at the women in cinema and drama, these men look at their wives and say that they look like old hags.'

Kannagi actually said this in a low voice, but somehow Andaal heard it and broke into laughter.

'After three children, you are only an old hag. What do you think, you are still a maiden?' This annoyed Kannagi.

'Let me be an old hag. Am I going to come of age now and get married as a young bride?' Just then a woman passed by and stepped on Kannagi's foot.

'Where does she have her eyes? Look at her, she is not even aware she stamped on my foot. Does not look where she is going, her eyes are on the TV. Cursed woman.' But that woman did not even hear Kannagi abusing her. Instead, she walked towards the casuarina barricade that separated the women and men.

'Look at the dancers' faces. How beautiful. Looks like I will cast an evil eye on them . . .' Before Andaal completed her words, Kannagi interrupted.

'Why do you say that? Why don't you say look at their breasts jutting like ripe coconuts? What do you lose? See where this old woman stares?' Kannagi loudly laughed.

'You really have a big mouth.' Andaal tapped her cheek affectionately.

'Look at the men's side. All of them are taking pictures on their cell phones. Do you think they are video-recording their dance? Naaaw! They are doing it to see their tits and their faces.'

'They are dancing only for all to see, isn't it?'

'Yeah, yeah.' Kannagi grimaced.

A schoolgirl sitting in the row in front of Andaal was video-recording the girls dancing on her cell phone. Looking at her, Andaal asked, 'How much will each of those girls be paid?'

'Surely it will be Rs 3000–4000 per head. Young girls, no? So, the rate will be high.' Kannagi winked.

'Every day?'

'I think they will dance in every town daily until the elections are over.' Kannagi spread her sari ends and fanned herself.

'Why can't they hold meetings without the dance? Why should they make such young girls dance in party meetings?' Andaal asked naively, like a child.

'It is to gather the crowd and make sure they don't disperse, of course,' Kannagi commented drolly.

'Is it proper to let young girls dance in party meetings in revealing costumes?'

'It is happening right in your presence,' Kannagi laughed.

'Is this performance only here or in every town?'

'In every town. The crowd comes only to gape at these young women. Otherwise, how will they muster crowds?'

'It is only to fill their stomachs that these girls dance like this before such crowds, bending and twisting, lifting their hands and feet and spreading themselves.'

Before Andaal could finish, Kannagi interrupted, 'Why don't you plainly say that they are jiggling their breasts and revealing almost half as they dance? Why are you hiding what you think? It is only so that all the people and the whole world should see that they make these girls wear transparent clothes that hide nothing.' Kannagi laughed loudly.

'Your mouth is as wide as Sembaiyanar Temple Lake.' Andaal laughed gently.

'These dancers dance for the sake of their stomachs. That is the same reason why we have come here in this horrible sun and are sitting in the middle of this huge crowd,' Kannagi looked for someone among the men as she spoke.

'We must do what we are destined to and we must bear the experience also,' Andaal said softly as though she was speaking to herself.

'Keep this seat for me. I'll come back now. Let no one sit there.' Kannagi walked swiftly towards the men's enclosure.

'Where is she going in this crowd? If she gets caught in the rush, they will stamp on her like they stamp on cow dung,' Sornam commented.

Andaal held on to Kannagi's chair to prevent anyone else from sitting there.

'Usually, we have summer rains around this time. This year there has not been even a drizzle.' While Andaal was speaking, Kannagi rushed back to her chair.

'I saw people from my mother's place. That is why I went. It seems two vans coming to this meeting collided with each other. One man is dead. Those people were going only to see what happened. They don't know who died—maybe our relatives. If my mother calls, I'll have to go for the condolence. Bereavement in my birthplace, how can I not go? I am caught in this crowd like it is an inescapable crisis,' she said and quickly called her husband.

'It seems some man from my mother's place died in the van accident. If they inform us, will you go and see the bereaved people?'

Andaal grimaced at the young girls dancing on stage.

'Look at them dancing in front of so many people. No shame, nothing.'

'If they are paid, they will dance in the nude.'

'Even for that, isn't there a limit? Look at them, shameless creatures.'

'The men are panting only to stare at these young women. See, see—how they are taking videos on their cell phones!'

Enthused by the sight of the girls dancing on the stage, four women were dancing like them ten or twelve rows away. A small crowd had collected to see them as well.

'Look at them dancing in this hot sun.' Kannagi laughed while pointing at them. Andaal and Sornam joined in the laughter.

'The swagger of flesh,' Andaal observed at the sight.

'It is one thing if young people dance but see those older women. Just look at them.' Kannagi was amused.

Some of the women who were watching the dancers started clapping. The dancers continued with more vigour when they saw that the crowd was watching them. The women rose from their chairs to see the dance.

'Do these bitches look like they are dancing in the midday sun? Are they at some wedding party to prance like this? Not an ounce of shame in their bodies when men are gazing at them.' Andaal spat in disgust.

'The one who wants to dance, dances. What's your problem? You just watch the fun. They dance only to get the men to look at them,' Kannagi told her.

'Isn't there a place to dance? And a limit?'

'Old women like you must not be brought to such places,' Kannagi teased her. Andaal was provoked by her words and felt insulted.

'We have also seen dance in olden times, was it like this? Lifting your skirt and showing is dancing, is it?'

'It is money in hand and a feast for the eyes. This is why they set out with full make-up when asked to come to a party meeting,' Kannagi replied and continued as though it was a very confidential matter, 'Other things are happening behind the scenes, you won't understand.' She winked at Andaal.

'These women are dancing like the ones on the stage,' Sornam exclaimed.

'These are shameless times,' Andaal said.

12

Venkatesa Perumal came with two men, pushing and shoving the crowd. He was carrying a huge polythene bag, from which he took out caps with the picture of the TUMK leader. He distributed the caps—one for each person.

'Our leader's cap must be on everyone's head,' he ordered. The little girls asked for more caps, but he said that only one cap would be given per person. He then handed over the remaining caps to the two men along with the bag.

'Distribute them to our town people. You must also give to the colony people. Don't give two caps to anyone,' he warned.

The little girls and the young women alone wore the caps. When Venkatesa Perumal saw the other women holding the caps in their hands, he shouted, 'Why are you all keeping it in your hands? Wear the caps now. Look around. Are they all holding the caps in their hands? Aren't they wearing the caps?' On hearing this, some women put the caps on. When he saw some women like Gomathi, Chellammal, Sornam, Kannagi and Andaal were still not wearing the caps, he threatened them, 'Are you going to wear the caps or . . .?'

'Won't we feel shy?' Kannagi asked.

'Why shy? It will shade you from the sun. Wear it, *anniyaa*.'

She then wore it with a shy smile. Two other women who had not worn the caps also put them on. As soon as they wore it, Andaal and Sornam burst into laughter. They were also overcome with shyness.

'Your leader . . . when will she come?' Andaal asked.

'In fifteen minutes to half an hour.'

'It is very hot. We feel thirsty. Please give us water packets.'

'When our leader arrives, all the caps must be on your heads. Understand?'

Instead of responding to this, Andaal said, 'You first bring us water.' Kannagi and Sornam joined in her request.

'Let me see,' he said and left.

'He chants "our leader, our leader" as though it is the name of some god,' Sornam said and Andaal grimaced.

'Not for nothing does he do it. It is all for cash, for money.'

Kannagi, who was sitting to the right of Andaal, sneered, 'Without that leader lady, where will he get this white shirt and white *veshti*?'

'It is because he went after the party all the time that he has managed to buy a car, build a huge house and become the town's big shot.' Sornam sounded envious.

'The one who fell at their feet got rich. In his party, the more you fall at the feet, the more money and power,' Kannagi mocked.

'Whether she gave money or power, didn't she make all the men in the country fall at her feet? For that alone, I like that lady. It is for this reason I vote for that party,' Kannagi bragged.

'Afraid that she will wilt in the sun, he has not brought his wife here and left her sitting at home. Instead, he has brought us all to roast while sitting in this sun,' Andaal said.

'Why will he bring his wife here? She will become dark, no?' Kannagi was a little angry.

'His mother got married and came to our town the year after I was married. At that time, did they have a house or any property? Not even a place to cook their meals. They were like these homeless wanderers who cook and eat under the shade of the tamarind tree. His parents roamed around every street waiting for someone or the other to call them to gather cashew nuts. But now . . . see . . . good times have come. And they preen around. Don't we all know the early story? His wife now comes out only if her hair is well-combed, sari is without a single wrinkle and the make-up on her face is fresh,' Sornam made a long speech.

Wasn't this fellow totally idle, without any work, always drunk and playing cards in front of the Chelliamman temple?' Andaal added.

The people of Chinna Kandiyankuppam may have accepted Venkatesa Perumal but they would never accept his wife, Karpagam. At least he would buy a coffee or tea for the party people. With her, you wouldn't even get a drop of water to wipe your mouth after eating. She also belonged to this town . . . born, brought up and married, everything was here. Her parents Veeran and Sembayi had four children— all girls. The first one got married and settled in Kovilanur, the second one in Chitherikuppam and the third one in Periya Vadavadi. Karpagam, the fourth and the youngest, married Venkatesa Perumal. All the girls got married at Sembayanaar temple in one of those 'free' weddings. At the time of the marriage, the earrings Karpagam wore were so flimsy that they would have floated in the wind and the nose ring . . . you had to search where it was. The only ornaments that were visible to all were her anklets which were as large as a cow's bells. When she walked, you knew it was Karpagam by the jingle of her anklets. She had gone to work at the cashew plantation even on the days before and after the wedding. But now . . . she did not take a step outside the house. If she went somewhere, it would only be in the Tata Sumo. She would be decked in gold chains and gold bangles, not just for temple or out-of-town visits, but even when she was just sitting at home. Be it morning or evening, her face would be powdered, the flowers on her hair would always be fresh and never faded, and the sari she would wear would be without a wrinkle. She always looked as though she had bridal make-up on. She never came out unnecessarily. At her bidding, it was only her mother-in-law who drew the rice flour *kolams* in front of the house.

You could not find a single female in Chinna Kandiyankuppam who did not fume against Karpagam. And when they cursed her, she alone was not targeted as they would curse her husband and the leader of TUMK too.

'True, good times have come, but should it be like this, that she does not know if she is standing on her head or her feet? Even the wife of the Seth, the Gujarati jeweller who owns the biggest jewellery shop in Vriddhachalam, will not strut around covered in gold like her. But no point in blaming her. It is that lady, the leader of her husband's party, who must be blamed. To hide the wealth she has stashed away, she has let her party-men loot the funds as they please. That is why her party-men and their wives dance around, unaware if it is day or night or if it is their belly or bum.'

When each of them started talking about Venkatesa Perumal and his family, Sornam was filled with anger against her sons.

Sornam's first son, Rajendran, was a member
of the Uzhaippali party, which was his caste party.
Her second son, Sakthivel, belonged to the party
that proclaimed there was no god. The third son,
Murugavel, was in a newly formed party 'Therdalai
purakanippom', that wanted to boycott elections.
The three of them were always after their party but
would always end up spending out of their pockets.
Not one had even Rs 10 to show that they had earned
from their party. They knew fully well that their party
would never ever come to power. Then why did they
hang around the party?

Everyone knew that only TUMK and UTMK people
got power and prosperity, and that money poured in
only in Venkatesa Perumal's party. Sornam was filled
with gripe that her sons were not in the money-making
parties but where they had to spend their own money.
In her anger, she abused them.

'The ones who are now strutting and lecturing
from platforms were just small grubby worms then.
The ones who did not even have a change of clothes
to wear, who did not know where to look for the next
day's gruel, now announce they are royalty. And I . . .
I have three sons. Good-for-nothings who have joined
worthless parties. They have no plan to join another
party and earn some money. Instead, they are scraping
what is at home and throwing it on the party. It must
have been a good time when Venkatesa Perumal's
father bedded his wife—his son is cheered by the town

and the whole world as he wallows in wealth. Our children were born at some wretched time, so we are roasting in this sun. This too is written in our fate.'

When Kannagi heard Sornam venting her frustration about her sons who had not made even one rupee from the party, she remembered her husband who hadn't earned anything either. She began to rail against him.

'I too have one stupid fellow as my husband . . . what use is he? He has no time even to lie next to his wife, running around all the time, day and night. But has he made even Rs 10? No. If my husband is worth just a tamarind seed, his children are worse . . . not even a neem seed. No benefit for me . . . not even a fistful of salt . . . from him or his children. Venkatesa Perumal's wife was born under a different star. For just a piddling Rs 500, here I am under the sun, sitting as if on a furnace. But this is my birth star. Even the money I got for coming here, this husband of mine snatched from me.' Kannagi was fed up.

'Didn't Venkatesa Perumal stash away the entire compensation given to him for all the cashew trees that were felled by the hurricane four months ago?' Andaal accused. Sornam replied, adding fuel to it.

'Not just here, everywhere else too. It was only these party-men who swallowed and wiped clean what was given by the government.'

'Was it only the hurricane relief money that they swallowed? Out of the Rs 3 lakh that is given to all to build houses, they stash away Rs 1 lakh for this or that and only hand over the balance.'

'Only if they do things like that, can they ride around in cars and feast in hotels.'

'If the hurricane had not flattened my cashew trees, would I be sitting here in the sun for Rs 500? Only now I have planted fresh saplings. They must first grow and then the cashew must come, and then I can see the cash. Until then, life is only a struggle.' Andaal was talking about the hurricane that had come four or five years before, which uprooted all the cashew trees, rendering them waste. Kannagi interrupted her.

'Now, it is not like before. Anything that is given by the government is deposited in the bank. Party people cannot steal anything. You know very well that they ask for your Aadhar card even if you want to piss.'

Andaal went on and on about her cashew trees, shedding tears now and then. She did not really listen to what Kannagi was saying.

'I tended to each tree as if it was my child. And this hurricane pulled them all from their roots and dashed them down in just fifteen minutes.'

'All the trees in the entire village got uprooted, not just yours,' Sornam said.

Kannagi saw Venkatesa Perumal at a distance walking towards them.

'That fellow is coming.' At once Sornam and Andaal stopped talking about him and acted as if they were looking at the women in the nearby rows.

13

Venkatesa Perumal brought a fertilizer sack full of water packets and gave everyone two packets each. Some of them drank the water immediately and asked for more. He glared at them in response.

'Only two per person. I have to give everyone, is it not?'

Just then, two men from their town came. One of them carried badges on which the TUMK leader's face was printed. The other carried small flags on which also her face was printed. Venkatesa Perumal first distributed one badge each amongst them. Then he distributed the flags along with small pins to pin the badges on their chests. At first, only the young girls wore the badges. The older ones were reluctant at first, but he compelled them to wear it. Then he showed them all how to hold the flags.

'It is enough if you hold the flags when our leader comes, then when she speaks and then when she leaves. The cap must be on your heads and the flag must be in your hands. If not, I'll get very angry. You must not remove your cap or put the flag down,' he said in an ordering tone. Just then three or four kids waved the flags this way and that and laughed.

'Be careful, you may poke somebody's eyes,' he warned them. The badge fell off Sornam's granddaughter Gayatri's blouse.

'First, fasten it properly,' he said.

'When will your leader come?' Andaal asked.

'Very soon.'

'You've been saying the same thing ever since we came here.' Andaal grimaced and Venkatesa Perumal immediately replied as though saying something very important, 'Didn't you hear what they announced on the mic?'

'Those mic-set fellows have been repeating since morning that she is coming just now.'

Venkatesa Perumal ignored her remark.

'Did you see the huge crowd that has come to see my leader? Just wait and see how many people will keep coming.'

But Venkatesa Perumal spoke the truth. The women and girls of Chinna Kandiyankuppam had never seen so many people before and speculated about the number of people in this country. Not just the crowd but even the din raised by the crowd aroused a never-before joy and energy in everyone's mind and body. As they kept looking at the crowd, flags, festoons, digital banners and cut-outs, the women and girls of Chinna Kandiyankuppam thought that it was only their good fortune that had brought them here. Andaal saw the TUMK leader's face on the flags stuck on iron rods planted in rows and on the buntings, digital banners and cut-outs that were strung around the meeting stage, and murmured, 'She is really a wondrous being.'

It was an unparalleled sight to see the flags, caps and badges—all bearing the leader's picture—in everyone's hands.

While Venkatesa Perumal was talking to Andaal, Sornam's granddaughter Gayatri and Chellammal's daughter Deepika came up to him and asked, 'Is there a bathroom somewhere?'

'All those things won't be here. Even if there is, you can't go anywhere in this crowd. Don't go here and there, you'll get lost,' Venkatesa Perumal snapped.

'No toilets for women?' Sornam asked him.

'I really don't know.'

'Where will so many women relieve themselves?' she asked sharply.

'I don't think there is any such facility but let me find out.' Venkatesa Perumal left on that note.

14

'Let us go somewhere *aayah*,' Gayatri called her grandmother Sornam as she wanted to pee.

'How can we go out in this crowd?'

'Let us go. It is urgent.'

'If we go out, the crowd will crush us to death. Just squat and do it.'

'You have no shame at all,' Gayatri said and returned with Deepika to her chair.

'There are banners and cut-outs as long as ten towns. And a stage as big as a village, a huge TV on which you can see the whole street. They have dragged all the people in this country by van, bus or car, stacked like cattle and goats and dumped them here. But what is the use? There is not an inch of place that is secluded for women to pee. What party are they running?' Sornam cursed the party-men. Andaal replied at once.

'These fellows just lift their veshti and do it like dogs do in the streets by lifting a leg. So how will they know what problems women will face?'

'The wretches who do not provide for a women's toilet roam around to see when a woman will lift her sari. Isn't it to see just that these men loaf around day and night?' Sornam grimaced.

'The whole world revolves only around that, no?' Andaal said when the loudspeaker blared.

'Golden leader, glorious leader,
The whole world praises her
The soil of Tamizhagam turned gold,
Under her rule so brave and bold
The goddess whom we worship,
The goddess of all goddesses
Long live, live long.'

This song blared from all the huge loudspeakers and the racket seemed to tear their eardrums.

A totally inebriated man staggered from the men's enclosure and came near the women singing, 'Golden leader, glorious leader.' A woman who was sitting near the barricade was afraid that he might fall on her in his drunken stupor.

'Scum, on whom are you going to fall? If I kick, both your balls will be punctured!' She gave him a push. He tottered as though he may fall but did not.

He walked on, staggering and quite unaware of the
fact that a woman had abused him with these words.

Watching that woman and the drunken fellow,
Kannagi noted, 'These drunken trash deserve only
this.'

'Wash your mouth, chee,' Sornam chided Kannagi.

'It is sizzling hot and feels as if we are on fire. I
wonder how he can drink the *saarayam*.'

'There isn't enough water for us but from
somewhere, these drunks get their country liquor.'
Kannagi bemoaned and a woman sitting behind said
in a teasing tone, 'Didn't you see when they came with
the fertilizer bag distributing water packets, two or
three men came selling liquor sachets?' Kannagi turned
round at once.

'It will be a blessing for women if they shut down
all the liquor shops,' that woman said and Kannagi
said in a sing-song mocking voice, 'The leader is also
a woman, but the liquor shops have not been closed.'

That woman replied to this, sounding sharp as if
a small stone was flung on a stone slab, 'Wasn't it she
who opened a shop in every street and every village?'

'Which town?' Kannagi asked her.

'Nallur.'

'Come from so far away?'

'Not just me, my whole town has come.' The
woman laughed and continued, 'Not for nothing
though—they gave each of us a sari, a biryani packet
and Rs 500.'

The Nallur woman must have been less than thirty. The way she spoke and laughed made her sound like a young girl. Kannagi liked her at once.

She started talking to the Nallur woman.

15

Andaal thought that she was perspiring more only because she was wearing a cap. So, she removed it and wiped the trickling sweat from her forehead and neck. As she fanned herself with the cap, she looked closely at the flag she held in her left hand. On a plastic with a circumference of roughly 1 ft, they had printed the TUMK leader's face. They had stuck this on a 2- or 3-foot-long bamboo stick and nailed it. 'Neither the bamboo stick nor the face of the leader printed on the plastic can be easily broken,' thought Andaal.

'Her face shines like gold,' she said, looking at the leader's face.

'Why will her face go dark? Does she have to cut the branches in the sun or pick up the cashew nuts like us? It seems like even her toilet has an AC. If one has to be born a woman, it must be like her. Here we are also born as women, only to cut branches and chop brinjals.' Kannagi frowned.

'Aayah, let us go, it is coming urgently,' Sornam's granddaughter Gayatri whimpered. Sornam stood up to see if she could find a way out.

She realized that from the time they had got out of the van, the crowd had increased tenfold. There was a huge crowd actually standing in the passage for entry and exit that was bigger than the crowd that sat inside the enclosures. Sornam doubted very much if she would be able to return once she went out.

'If we go out, they will stamp on us as if we are cow dung. I have no clue which way to go and which way to return.'

'Urgent Aayah, it is coming.' Gayatri started crying.

'Spread your skirt, squat and do it.'

'Let us go out.'

'All of us here are women only. Squat. By the time you wink your eye, it will come out.' Gayatri did not agree even though Sornam tried to persuade her. So, she turned behind and called Chellammal who was sitting three rows behind, 'Hey, your daughter wanted to go, did she?'

'I told her then itself to squat here and piss.' When Sornam heard Chellammal say this, she again asked Gayatri to do it right there.

Just then Gomathi said, 'I too want to go, I will take her.'

As she started walking along with Gayatri, three or four women also followed her.

16

Gomathi and the others who went in search of a toilet returned very soon.

'Did the job?' Kannagi asked.

'We couldn't go out as it was too crowded. Curse them. It seems there is no toilet for women. The only outcome for trying to go and have a pee is that my hundred-rupee-slipper got torn.' Gomathi sounded fed up.

'What happened?'

'Even as we were going, someone stamped on my foot. When I pulled free, the strap broke.' Andaal was surprised to hear her talk of it as if it was someone else's slippers.

'She doesn't seem affected at the loss of a hundred rupees,' Andaal thought.

'I stooped to pick up my slippers. That was it. The milling crowd kept pushing me further and further away.' She smiled.

'So hundred rupees gone down the drain?' Kannagi teased.

'At least for me it was a hundred-rupee-slipper. One woman lost her chain.'

'How did that happen?' Kannagi, Andaal and Sornam asked in one voice.

'No one knows who cut the chain from her neck. It broke my heart to see her weep, beating her chest at the loss of her chain.' Gomathi's face changed as she narrated it. Her heart melted even for simple things, though to look at, she was stout and short. Everyone in Chinna Kandiyankuppam thought she was a good sort.

'From which town was she?'

'Don't know.'

'How many sovereigns was the chain?' Andaal was eager to know.

'Don't know. I stopped just for a moment, a blink of an eye. The crowd pushed me away like the river sweeps away the clothes on the banks. It was more than enough to return safely from this crowd. I wondered why I even left this place at all. Oh god! What a crowd! And what a crush! On the way, there were so many people. I could neither go out nor come back. Hereafter we must not come for such meetings. It won't be easy to go out even after the meeting is over.' To hear Gomathi, it sounded really as though she had escaped from a big danger.

'Shouldn't she have known that the chain might get lost in a crowd?' Andaal asked.

'They come fully decked only to show off to others,' was Kannagi's cynical comment.

'But now she has lost what she had, no?' Sornam said. Kannagi just smiled without saying anything.

'It is one thing to steal something when no one is there. But to cut the chain round the neck is so sinful.' Gomathi sounded sad.

'Wretched woman has lost a chain worth god knows how many sovereigns, just for this piddling Rs 500,' Andaal said.

'Losing the chain is not a big thing, compared to what she may face at home. How much she may be beaten by her husband and how many quarrels she may have to face.' Gomathi sounded as if she truly felt for the woman who had lost her chain.

'The moment someone asks people to come for a meeting, hordes come from every village. And do they look as if they are coming for a political meeting? No, they come decked as if they are going to a wedding.' Kannagi was annoyed.

Sornam, Kannagi and Andaal joined Gomathi in the conversation about not just the woman who lost her chain, but also all the women who had come for the meeting and how they had adorned themselves.

17

'It is a big mistake to have chosen to sit in a corner.' Sornam was tired.

'That we got a place to sit is a blessing. If we had come just a little while later, we would not have gotten even this. We would have been crushed to death, in the passage or near the barricade,' Andaal spoke as if getting a seat was like finding a treasure.

Sornam saw some women smiling and talking to the men who stood near the barricade, and she commented to no one in particular, 'Why can't these bitches sit in one place in the meeting. Why go and parade in front of the men?'

Before Andaal could reply, Kannagi burst with laughter and said insinuatingly, 'Only to be noticed by all.'

'But should they do this in this big crowd?' Sornam asked loudly.

Kannagi understood why Sornam had raised her voice, but she said with a snide smile, 'If there are cows, will they not move towards the bull? It is natural, isn't it?'

'I can understand if a cow that has not calved even once moves close to the bulls. But even cows with three or four calves are prancing around.' Kannagi could not hold back her laughter when Sornam said this. She forgot that she was in a crowd and there were people all around and laughed loudly. Andaal and Sornam joined her.

'Whichever cow it may be—until it calves two or three times, it is bound to roam around,' Sornam said.

'What do the young calves know? They just go about to graze. It is only the mature cows who will know what is what. But see there, the cows who have calved twice or thrice are showing off more than the young ones. And what is more, the cows whose udders have dried are going round in circles.' Kannagi pointed to the women who were simpering at the men near the barricade.

'Be careful, someone may hear what you say or notice you,' Andaal warned Kannagi, who did not pay the slightest heed and continued to make fun of the women who were chatting up the men or parading up and down.

Kannagi was less than forty. She was born in Anguchettipalayam near Panruti. She had three children—two girls and a boy. You wouldn't say she was a mother of three looking at her. She was very slim, with skin like a coat of paint on the wall. But her mouth . . . as wide as the Sembaiyanar Kovil lake.

Whether on the street or working in the fields, if the women wanted to be entertained, they would egg Kannagi on to talk. She would pepper her talk with comments about sexual affairs or sexual descriptions. Every word she uttered would have a double meaning. Sometimes, what she said would have a subtext and sometimes it would be coarse. She would effortlessly and without any inhibitions, use bad words. You could not find one person in Chinna Kandiyankuppam without a nickname given by her. Just as she gave everyone in town a nickname, the townspeople jointly gave her the title, 'A mouth that carries loads'.

People felt Kannagi's words were like firecrackers but still could not help laughing at her comments. Though Kannagi spoke vulgarly and coarsely, she would never gossip, quarrel or speak ill of anyone. Andaal liked Kannagi very much. If she needed an extra hand at home or in the field, the first person she asked was Kannagi.

18

'They said the lady would come at ten itself. But no sign of her. And it is boiling hot,' Sornam said to Andaal, who was tired and fanning herself with her sari.

'Hasn't your son come?'

'His second son has been with a fever for the last four days and showing no signs of getting better. I told my son to take the child to the hospital. What happened to your son-in-law?' When Sornam asked her this, Andaal's face changed. She forgot the dust, humidity, heat and sweat, and began to abuse her son-in-law, Senthil Kumar.

'That drunk left home six months ago deserting his wife and child, you know that story.'

'Are you going to leave it just like that without doing anything about it?'

'That fellow . . . he is now running around with that woman who has been appointed as the *thalaiyari*. How will he come back?'

'Are they now appointing women as village assistants?'

'Oh, yes. They have appointed a widow as the village assistant in Reddikuppam. He is now her odd-jobs man, drinking her piss.' Andaal's voice was filled with resentment.

'He will get married, give her two children and then coolly walk off with another woman, and you will let him do it?' Sornam was angry.

'If she asks him, he beats her black and blue and verbally abuses her. Once he asked her to make a claim on our house and our lands. He then beat her saying she could go to her mother's house if she was not willing to do it. Unable to bear the violence, she came away and that was it. I tried two or three times to make peace but he does not seem amenable to reason. He is now caught in the net of this new woman. Piss-drinker,' Andaal spat out her words.

'Tell four or five people in the village and try to mediate.' Sornam was concerned.

'Is there anything you don't know? I gave my daughter to him thinking he would be the head of the family as I had no husband and no sons. It is he who has driven us to this position.' Andaal was in tears.

'Why do you cry now, in this blazing heat?' Kannagi sitting near her consoled her.

'If there had been a father or a brother, younger or older, would they have let him do as he pleases?' Andaal said to herself. She really believed that if her husband

Ganapathi was alive, her daughter Valarmathi would not have suffered so much, nor would she be sitting in the hot sun at a political party meeting for some cash.

Andaal was born in Periya Kandiyankuppam and Ganapathi, in Chinna Kandiyankuppam. The two towns were not even one mile apart and were only separated by the Sembaiyanar Lake—Periya Kandiyankuppam was on the north bank of the lake and Chinna Kandiyankuppam was on the south bank. When she got married and came over, she was not even twenty years old.

Andaal was an only child and so was her husband Ganapathi. Their child Valarmathi was also an only child. When she was studying in the eighth standard, lightning struck Ganapathi, who was grazing cattle in the cashew grove, and killed him. From that day onwards, Andaal stopped rearing cattle and goats. After Valarmathi came of age, not once did Andaal hit her or speak a harsh word. She did not even send her daughter to their own cashew grove to pick the nuts or let her shell the nuts at home.

'If she goes to the fields, my child's complexion will grow dull, if she shells the nuts, her hands will get sore,' she would say. 'I brought her up by not letting anything harm or hurt her and handed her over to a butcher,' she thought.

'Did I do anything less for her marriage? I gave her six sovereigns of gold jewellery that were adorning her nose and ears. I gave all that I had when I gave her in marriage. The rascal squandered all of that and now wants the cashew grove to spend on his keep. To hell with him.' If she abused Senthil Kumar this much, she abused Ezhilarasi a hundred times more.

'They have named this stinking shit Ezhilarasi, meaning beauty queen. Is she a woman who sets fire to another woman's house? Why these dancing whores who have lost all sense of shame make a glittering spectacle of themselves wearing saris, I don't know. It seems like it is only such sluts who have good fortune nowadays,' Andaal wailed.

'You wail and rail like this, why can't you call the panchayat and ask for justice?' Sornam asked impatiently but Andaal brushed her off saying, 'In these days, which fellow abides by the panchayat's decision?'

'If it is not the town panchayat, call the caste panchayat or go to the police station. You know, now there are all-women police stations. And women too, run there straight and ask them to dissolve the marriage saying they will not live with their spouse.'

'It can be done . . . but then he might say "you took me to the police station, so I will not live with you" and divorce her. Then what to do?' Tears spilled down Andaal's cheeks. 'This is the problem. These days, people go round claiming they won't abide by what the town people say or the caste people nor any panchayat.'

'Our days were a lot better. We were in our parents' house or our husband's house, this one or that one, that was all. See now, children who do not even know to piss or poo, travel 50–60 km to attend school. Young women, about twenty or thirty, go around in cars every day. The days are like that. They are not afraid of their parents or their partner, nor of what the townspeople will say.'

'Yes . . . yes. No fear, no inhibition at all. No one wants anyone.'

Sornam and Andaal were talking like they would if they were at home shelling cashew nuts.

19

'It is past twelve. If it is going to be this late, why did that wretched fellow drag us here in the morning itself? My head will burst in this heat.' Chellammal started cursing Venkatesa Perumal, and every woman in her row followed her and did the same.

'He has tied and brought us here like cattle and goats are taken to slaughter.' Andaal was annoyed with him. She felt that she would not have felt so exhausted even if she had shelled cashew nuts all day or picked them in the grove. On the one side, it was the scorching heat and on the other, it was the thirst, the crowd, noise, dust and inability to go somewhere to pee, and having to sit in the same place for so long. All this made her feel exhausted and her head ached. At least if she was at home, she could have rubbed pain balm on it. She looked at the women on both sides—dust covered their faces like powder on school-going children. Even the fair-skinned Kannagi looked dark.

As time passed, Andaal got very tired.

'When will that woman arrive, when will I go home?' she mumbled. Just then the woman sitting behind Sornam shouted, '*Ayyo*, my purse is gone,' and started wailing and hitting her head. Andaal turned round and looked at her with sympathy.

'The heat is scorching and because we are sitting in the crowd, it feels like a weight on us,' Kannagi said and started fanning herself with her cap. The enthusiasm with which they had all gotten into the van, and the excitement when they saw the digital banners, cut-outs, crowd, the decorated dais, vans and cars, slowly started waning. This was not so only for the Chinna Kandiyankuppam women as all the women there were exhausted. The women who had danced with gusto as soon as they had arrived there were quietly sitting down, exhausted. Every woman there, without exception, was fanning herself with either the cap or her sari. Being in the crowd made them all feel the heat more, but there was nowhere they could go from the crowd or stand for shade. To accommodate the crowd, all the trees in the 400–500 acres of land expanse had been cut. There was not a tree, plant or a creeper as far as the eye could see. All that could be seen were the party flags, festoons, cut-outs and digital banners.

Every woman and girl of Chinna Kandiyankuppam was cursing Venkatesa Perumal as though that was the only way to escape from this scorching heat, humidity and thirst. Some women called him on the phone and shouted that they wanted water. To everyone, his only response was, 'Coming now.'

One hour went by, then two hours . . . but there was no sight of the TUMK leader or Venkatesa Perumal. The infuriated women called him again and again.

'Why hasn't your leader arrived yet?'

'Why don't you answer the phone?'

'Come and sit with us here in this blazing heat, then you will know.'

'Why did you bring us here so early in the morning?'

'We want lunch now.'

The women took turns screaming at him over the phone.

20

Venkatesa Perumal arrived with another man at 2.15 p.m. and distributed one food packet with one water sachet to each person.

'Why did you bring us here this early?'

'How long to sit here in this sun?'

'We want none of this rubbish to eat.' The women began fighting and he tried to pacify them.

'What can I do? I am doing only what my district head or the panchayat head says. Can we ask our leader why she is so late? She will come when she comes and go when she goes.' He somehow pleaded and begged them to calm down, and some of the women started eating.

'Is this biryani or kuska?' Kannagi asked as soon as she began eating.

'Biryani, it is.'

'You say so, but I can't find even one piece of meat in it,' she said mischievously.

'Dig into it, there will be a piece.' Venkatesa Perumal then turned to the fellow who came with him carrying the food packets. 'Take the remaining packets and go give them to our town people. No one must complain that they did not get food.'

'What happened to the meat, did it get dried up? You must have taken money promising to distribute biryani and are now giving us this plain kuska. This is how that lady operates, making you all flatten yourself before her. You prostrate before the helicopter, even the tyre of her car. She treats you like a puppy dog but you won't change your ways,' Kannagi snapped.

'I only gave what the panchayat secretary handed over to me. Maybe he took money for biryani from the district head and palmed off the kuska.' Not just Kannagi, even the little girls from Chinna Kandiyankuppam did not believe what he said.

When the women started quarrelling with him for giving kuska, he diverted their attention by repeatedly asking them if anyone had been left out while distributing the packets.

'The kuska you gave did not even fill a quarter of our stomachs, go get us more,' Rasathi from the East Street shouted and everyone sitting in her row joined in and said, 'Food is not enough, get us more.'

Unable to bear their pestering, he said, 'Don't shout, I will go and find out.'

Just then, Munuswami's son, Ramasami, asked him for Rs 200.

'Why do you want it?' Venkatesa Perumal asked.

'You give me first, I'll tell you later.' It was clear that Ramasami was drunk.

'I don't have change, I will give you later.' But Ramasami was in no mood to listen to him.

'You give what you have to me, I'll get you the change,' Ramasami insisted.

'Please understand. What are you saying right in the middle of this crowd?' But Ramasami was adamant. So, Venkatesa Perumal glared at him and handed him the money.

The moment he got the money, Ramasami left without even uttering a word. Venkatesa Perumal cursed him.

'I am better off grazing pigs than gathering these crowds. In the olden days, were the party-men like this? They would give their lives for the party. The crowd would gather by itself for meetings. Even seven years ago, it was not so bad. But now everyone is a rascal. They call themselves party-men and strip your guts. They don't give you the time of the day unless they are paid money. If we have to bring them, we must give them a veshti, towel, liquor, food and also cash. On top of it, all of them want an AC car. At this rate, God knows what will happen to the party. Every party is the same. Whichever party leader's meeting it is, a crowd can be assembled only if we lure them with money and food and bring them in a hired van. All my fate.' He hit his head with his hand in disgust.

'If a drunk demands cash you give, will you give us if we ask?' Kannagi asked while making faces at him.

The women began shouting for more food after Ramasami left. Venkatesa Perumal left the place saying he would find out if there was food.

'A big cheat,' Andaal said.

'If he was not one, how could he buy a car and a big house?' Kannagi retorted.

21

Venkatesa Perumal returned with seven or eight more food packets. The women hastily snatched them—he did not even know who got them.

'All the other town people have got biryani. Why did you give only us this wretched kuska?' Rasathi shouted holding one packet.

'They swindle even in food,' Nadu Street Vaanakkannan's wife Alamelu said.

'Isn't there meat even in one packet?' Venkatesa Perumal asked, feigning innocence.

'I don't want your biryani or any shit. First, give us some water to drink,' Rasathi said.

Venkatesa Perumal wanted to escape from these women's nagging. So, he tried to leave saying, 'Don't shout. I'll ask.'

'You first tell us when the leader will come. You brought us saying she will come at ten. What is the time

now? Tell us the truth. When will she come?' Kannagi
stopped him and asked, and all the others including
Sornam, Andaal and Gomathi joined in.

'Don't shout. Just listen to me. She will come in five
or ten minutes. When our leader finishes her speech,
the crowd will disperse, you all don't go with them.
Until I return, you stay here. If you get scattered in the
crowd, it will not be easy to collect you all and put you
in the van. It will then be very late when we go home,'
he warned them and then went to the men's side.

'When he asks us to come for the meeting, he speaks
one way, and after we are all here, his tone changes.
Shameless creature,' Alamelu cursed him.

'What can he do if that lady does not come? Who
knows how busy she is?' Andaal said, and Alamelu
snapped at once, 'Shouldn't she know that such a big
crowd is waiting here?'

'Go back to your place, you are speaking as though
I stopped that lady from coming here on time.' Andaal
glared at her and Alamelu returned to her seat in the
row behind.

'When will the lady be here? When will she finish
her speech? And when will we return home? No one
knows. That cursed fellow brought us here so early.
And holding on without peeing has given me a pee-
cramp too,' Andaal moaned.

'I told my grandson to give water to the cow and
clean the shed if I was late. Don't know whether the
dumb fool has done as I said or if he is loitering along

the banks of the lake playing cricket. Curse him,' Sornam blasted her grandson.

Over and above the heat, thirst, sweat, dizziness and headache, there was one thought that sat heavily on Andaal—whether Valarmathi had taken the child to the hospital or not.

22

'Oh, my dearest voters, who are more precious than my life, the body of my body, the eye of my eye, dearer than my life's breath, *vanakkam*, my greetings.' Andaal started to listen to the TUMK leader's recorded speech on the LED screen.

'I have never been for myself or lived for myself. I have always been for you and lived for you, for the people of Tamil Nadu. My rule is for the people. It is for the poor, the weak and the marginalized.

'Do you want a good government or a looting one?

'The people of other parties will act as though they are good only during the election times. Only at the time of the election, they will start thinking of our country. When they were in power, have they ever introduced a single good scheme? Apart from swindling and looting, what did they do? They know nothing except their own interest and their families'. Did they ever think about the people?'

Andaal was enthralled by her speech. She thought she could keep staring at the leader's face all day. She decided she would vote for her candidate just for the lady's looks, appearance and oration.

'Wow! What an oration!' On the stage, there must have been at least a hundred men. Andaal liked the way she spoke and went on, ignoring them and not even glancing at them, while all the men stood in absolute respect, hands folded. Her heart overflowed with joy.

'She is divine, not a mere mortal,' Andaal murmured.

As she went on listening to the TUMK leader's speech on the LED screen, her whole self and mind were filled with pride and joy.

'It is my ideal to make Tamil Nadu the foremost state in India. That is my dream. Will you vote for TUMK to make my ideal and my dream come true?' When she posed this question, the unanimous voice of the crowd could be heard.

'We will, we will.'

'When the other parties were in power, there was no educational growth, no economic self-sufficiency and no industrial development. The only thing that happened was corruption. But after I came to power, Tamil Nadu is in the first place in all spheres—education, employment, finance and industry. What did they do when they ruled? They only wanted power, pelf and position. That was their only goal. They are again daydreaming that they will somehow come to power again. Their dreams must be dashed.

'If TUMK comes to power again this time, I will create a golden Tamil Nadu and usher in a golden era in Tamil Nadu. Do you want a reign that works for the poor or a reign that aids the robbers?

'Can we let those who swindled, those who looted and those who made Tamil Nadu a burial ground, ascend the seat of power?

'For the country's welfare, for the continuance of good governance and welfare schemes for the people, the party you should support is TUMK. The party you should vote for and enable its victory is TUMK. Don't forget to vote for the TUMK candidates. Make them win. Long live the Tamils. Long live Tamil Nadu!'

Andaal had no clue who the TUMK leader was referring to as swindlers and robbers. She did not understand. But she liked the way the lady leader spoke. She liked her voice, which rang clear and true like the bronze bell in a temple. She liked the way the leader looked like a militant, shook her hands as though she would hit someone and spoke with a tone that seemed to throw a challenge. So, Andaal looked, without even blinking, at the leader's face seen on the LED screen and was amazed at how her words sounded. It was not just Andaal who felt this way and was rapt in amazement or the Chinna Kandiyankuppam women, but all the women who were there at the meeting.

The LED screen repeatedly showed the clip of the TUMK leader reading from a paper she held and delivering her speech at an election propaganda meeting.

'Why are these idle people showing the lady's speech again and again? If those girls who danced earlier are allowed to perform, at least it will be pleasant to the eyes and we won't feel the heat.' Andaal heard the Nallur woman's comment from behind.

23

Andaal looked up at the sky.

'It seems to be especially scorching today. In all my life, I have never experienced this heat. True, it is the summer season, but even so, the heat is too much. And these shameless fellows always fix the election dates only in this season.' She wiped the sweat on her face and fanned herself with the sari.

'What kind of woman is she? Doesn't she have any concern for the crowd that is waiting for her?' Kannagi said.

'Who cares for that? This huge crowd has been waiting from morning in this sun only to see her face,' Sornam replied.

'Maybe she has gone to speak at another meeting. She has to go to town after town before the elections and address the people, no?' Kannagi answered.

Andaal covered her face with the edge of her sari to shade it from the sun. Despite the cover, the sun hit her face. She could even bear the heat, but the humidity was intolerable. Over and above the heat and humidity, the cruellest was the thirst. An ordinary lunch would not have made her so parched—it was the biryani that had done it.

The women of Chinna Kandiyankuppam kept calling Venkatesa Perumal incessantly, asking for water. He kept saying, 'Coming, right away,' but neither he nor the water came.

'Oh! He won't answer now, is it? Let him come next time to invite me for a meeting, I'll give him hell,' Kannagi threatened.

As time passed, the heat kept rising and Andaal thought she should get out of the crowd. She looked to see if she could go out but it did not seem possible. The crowd had grown some ten or twentyfold since the morning. Andaal was filled with surprise to see the crowd that sat without dispersing, not minding the burning heat, and bearing patiently the dust, humidity, noise, crowd and the pouring sweat. Some women had come with babies in their arms. The laughter, joy, clamour and dancing that was there in the morning was not there now, but the crowd was there—it had not scattered even one bit. There was not one vacant chair in the men's enclosure, the women's enclosure or among the chairs in front of the dais. The passage was filled with twice as many people.

'What a mammoth crowd!' Andaal said and then sat back saying, 'If I try to go out in this crowd, I will be crushed to death.'

Andaal tried to wipe the perspiration that trickled from her forehead, but since the party sari that Venkatesa Perumal had given them was polyester, it could not absorb the moisture well. So, she wiped her forehead and neck with her hand. Her blouse and underskirt were drenched and the salty sweat had caked around her neck. She looked around—all the women around her were like her, dripping with sweat and salt-caked.

Andaal was feeling a little giddy. Sitting amidst the crowd was like sitting right in the middle of a sacrificial fire. More than the heat, humidity, thirst and dust, what was exhausting her was the non-stop chant from the loudspeakers, 'Thanga thalaiviye, dharma thalaiviye, golden leader, righteous leader.'

'This ear-splitting nonsense on top of everything,' she muttered. The sweat from her forehead fell and irritated her eyes. As she rubbed her eyes, she heard a scream from behind. The women in the row behind Alamelu and Rasathi's row were all standing up.

'What happened?' Andaal asked Rasathi.

'A young girl has fainted.'

At once, everyone in Andaal's row stood up. There was a lot of noise coming from where the girl had been sitting. Three women could be seen getting together to lift the child.

'Poor child, *paavam*,' Andaal said.

'In their greed for money, they have brought innocent kids here. Wait here, I'll go and see what happened. Don't let anyone take my chair, tell them it is occupied,' Kannagi said and went to the row where the girl was. In a short while, she came back.

'The girl is from Ponneri, it seems, studying in ninth standard.' She resumed her seat. For a while, she continued to talk about the Ponneri child and about people who bring young children to such meetings.

Andaal was restless, she could not even keep her eyes open. She felt giddier. She stretched her legs, leaned back in the chair and closed her eyes. Kannagi saw her face and the way she was sitting.

'What's wrong?'

'_____'

'Feel giddy, like fainting?'

'_____'

'Head spinning?'

'I regret coming to the meeting.'

'He brought some rubbish saying it is biryani. It is only after we had it that the throat feels parched . . . Will you have some water?' Kannagi asked her. Andaal nodded.

'Anyone has water?' she asked each one of the Chinna Kandiyankuppam women. No one had any. Then she asked the women in the nearby rows. It was only after much pleading, that 'a woman has fainted and needs water', that one woman from Irusalakkuppam relented and handed over a water packet she had hidden in her lap as though it was some treasure.

Kannagi returned with the packet of water.

'Water has become a rarity . . . here, drink some.' Kannagi gave the packet to Andaal, who looked at it with wonder.

'Drink it. It will make you feel a bit better.' Kannagi sounded concerned.

Andaal tried to pierce the packet with her teeth but she had no strength.

'Here, you make the hole and pour it in my mouth.'

Kannagi made a hole with her teeth and asked Andaal to open her mouth. She poured it into her mouth. It was like she was drinking boiling water—only half the water went into Andaal's mouth, the rest spilt out. If it had been a normal time, Andaal would not have drunk from a packet bitten by anyone else. 'You think I'll drink something sipped by you,' she would have railed at Kannagi. But now . . . now she did not even have the strength to open her mouth. Despite her weakness, she cursed Venkatesa Perumal.

'The murderer has brought us to sit in a fire.'

'If we had been working or walking, we wouldn't feel it so much. Even for *Agni Natchathiram*, the hottest days of summer, this is too much,' Kannagi said. Andaal cursed herself for getting lured by the offer of a sari and money. She felt that even if she had gone to pour tar in a road-laying work, this much heat would not have been there. She had not felt this heat even while laying concrete.

Usually, Venkatesa Perumal would collect people for a meeting and take them only in the evening. The meeting would be over by 9 or 10 p.m. and one could be home by 11 p.m. Andaal had gone for three political meetings and they had all been in the evening. They were propaganda meetings, welfare scheme distribution meetings and welcoming the ministers. There had not been even four or five hundred people on those occasions. This was the first time she had come for an election meeting during the day. If she had known it would take so long, she would not have come. If there had been some wind, the heat would not be so much. But even the mild wind that blew was scorching. She realized she had been trapped.

'When will that lady ever come?'

'Really don't know.' Kannagi sounded tired. She stood up when she heard a big shout from the men's side. Twenty or thirty rows behind, she could see a man being carried away by three men.

'A man is being carried away, don't know if he is dead or has fainted.' On hearing these words from Kannagi, Sornam and Gomathi stood up too.

'Impossible to say,' they said in one voice.

'Looks like this meeting will kill many,' Andaal moaned. She was not able to stand.

'Feel an awful pee-cramp. Both the thighs are burning. But where can I go and relieve myself? These witless people don't have the brains to put up an enclosure with a few coconut leaves for the women to go, what party are they running? What sort of meeting have they arranged?' Sornam complained and spread her sari out and squatted like a dog to pee.

'What happened?' Kannagi asked.

'The pee-cramp is unbearable.'

'The same story for me too, for the last hour. It feels like a block of fire is inside me,' Kannagi said and stood from the chair to squat like Sornam.

In every row, at least ten women did the same as Sornam and Kannagi.

24

At about 3.15 p.m., the sound of a helicopter whirring could be heard and at once, the whole crowd, every man and woman stood and shouted, 'Long live the golden leader, long live the righteous leader, long live the world leader.' The noise raised by them was so thunderous that it seemed as if the sky would fall and the entire place shook. At least 3 or 4 lakh people must have assembled and when all of them cheered, '*Vazhga vazhga*, long live, long live' at the same time, the din drowned the helicopter's sound. Everyone in the crowd looked up and not only cheered but also raised and waved the flags. The scattered crowd that was standing outside the men's and women's enclosures rushed in.

As soon as the TUMK leader's helicopter was heard, they started bursting crackers from all directions. The sound of the crackers was deafening like thunder and it also got the crowd excited. The sky was filled with the noise and smoke of crackers. Sornam stood up with the crowd to look at where the helicopter had landed and when she heard a 'Kaboom . . .' she trembled and closed her ears. Then she raised her hands and joined them in a namaste-like gesture, and shouted, 'Vazhga', as did the whole crowd.

The helicopter slowly descended to the ground. The leader came out and got into a car. The car moved majestically like a chariot and halted near the dais, where she got down. When she came up the dais, she folded her hands in a namaste to the crowd and then waved. The crowd shouted with all their strength, as though they had been waiting all this while only to see her wave.

'Long live the golden leader, long live the righteous leader, vazhga vazhga.'

Andaal gathered all the strength she had and shouted, 'Vazhga vazhga' as loud as possible.

One man kept shouting through the loudspeaker, 'Quiet, please', but no one listened to him.

25

It was possible to see the TUMK leader descending from the helicopter, getting into the car, climbing the dais and greeting the crowd on the LED screens. As though that was not enough, some men climbed up the casuarina barricades that separated the men's and women's enclosures. In a short while, the cracking sound of poles breaking could be heard. The men who had climbed on those poles for a distance of 100–200 m tumbled and fell on the women.

Caught among the broken poles, three women from Chinna Kandiyankuppam, a schoolgirl and a Nallur woman died. Another woman died because of the sharp edge of the stick of the party flag in her hand that pierced her intestines. Many people's limbs were broken. Many women screamed, 'Gone, gone', and hit their heads. Their laments could be heard making the women's side become very agitated. This intensified by the minute as people tried to lift the ones who were on the ground near the poles and there was a stampede. To escape from it, people tried to run and tripped and fell, and the crowd ran over them. This led to more confusion and agitation among the women.

People tried to flee as they would from a burning house, but the policemen beat them and sent them back into the enclosure. As there was more confusion, clamour and agitation among the women, the death count increased.

The TUMK leader knew nothing of what was happening among the women—the shouting, confusion, deaths or broken limbs. 'Oh, my dearest voters, who are more precious than my life, the body of my body, the eye of my eye, dearer than my life's breath, I have come to ask for your votes in the coming assembly elections for the TUMK candidates.' Unaware, she went on reading loudly from the paper in her hands.

Tiruneeru Sami

Annamalai was working on the computer as Varsha Pande looked at him.

'What are you doing in front of the computer for the last hour? And that too on a Sunday?'

He did not reply, nor did he look at her.

'Our son has gone to my mother's house. Will you bring him? Or should I go?' Varsha asked. Even then, he did not say a word.

'What are we doing for lunch? Are we eating out or at home?'

He still did not say a word.

She heard the cry of the baby in the bedroom. She rushed and came back with the infant. She spoke to the crying child, gave her a biscuit and water to drink, and tried to stop her crying. Then she boiled milk and gave the child the bottle. She spread out some toys, played with the child, and then asked Annamalai, 'Can you look after the child for a bit? I have to make lunch.'

'I'm a bit busy now.' He did not look at Varsha or the child even now.

'Don't I have to cook?' She came with the child and sat next to him. The child sprang towards the computer.

'Today is Sunday, it doesn't matter if you do it later.' His eyes remained focused on the computer screen.

'Is it something urgent?'

'Yes.'

'Can't you do it half an hour later?' She sounded as if she was pleading.

'Just ten minutes, Varsha. I'll finish this and come, please. I'm booking tickets.'

'Tickets to where? Baby, you can't touch the computer. Don't disturb Appa.' However, the child did not listen and was constantly stretching out to touch the computer.

'We are going to travel, Varsha.'

'Travel? Some holiday trip?'

'We are going to Tamil Nadu. To visit our family deity, our *kuladeivam*,' Annamalai replied, but his mind and eyes were focused on the computer.

'Why suddenly?' She stood up but the child did not stop reaching out to the computer.

'To perform the first tonsure for the children, to pierce their ears and to do the religious naming ceremony.'

'Should we do all that there only?'

'Yes,' he said emphatically.

'Can't we do it here itself?' she asked while playing with the child.

'It has to be done only in the kuladeivam temple, Varsha.'

'Should we go so far for that?'

'Yes.'

'I can't come all the way there.'

The child leapt into Annamalai's arms, and he held her.

'Do you know what you are doing?'

'Yes, that is why I am doing it.' He kissed the child.

'There is a limit to foolishness.' She sounded angry.

Annamalai did not say anything. He was looking at the child fondly.

'Will you have tea?' Without waiting for his answer, she went to the kitchen and turned the stove on to make tea.

He switched off the computer and began to play with the child. She brought two cups of tea and gave him one. Then she sat on the sofa and began to sip her tea.

'Have you bought the tickets?'

'Yes.'

'Shouldn't you ask if I have any urgent work?'

'I am not doing anything wrong.'

'I think what you did is wrong.' She was angry.

'You are a Delhi-born girl. There are things you don't know.'

'Doing tonsure is right but going to your home town for that is wrong.'

Varsha's voice showed that she was getting angrier—her face and voice clearly indicated the same.

He was not affected by it. In fact, he was happy . . . happy because he was going to his family temple.

'With regard to some matters, there is no right or wrong. Only once in a lifetime will we perform the tonsure, ear-piercing and naming ceremony for our child. That should be done in the kuladeivam temple. That is the custom.'

'All that is fine. My question is, should we go so far for this?'

'Even if it is across seven seas, we must go.'

'There are so many Tamil temples in Delhi itself, let us do it here.'

'Are you worried about the expense?'

'Don't be an idiot. I am thinking of the travel and the strain.'

'Just four days. From Delhi to Chennai by flight, then train and then car. Once the job is over, we will return.'

'It is all finalized, then?'

'Yes.'

Varsha did not say anything on hearing Annamalai's firm reply. She quickly went to the kitchen to prepare lunch.

Annamalai knew that she was simmering with anger and kept thinking that he must pacify her. But if he spoke to her now, she would lash out—better to wait for a day, he thought. He could hear her muttering while also banging vessels. If he waited for a day, she would get angrier. He decided to talk to her right away. He put the child down and went to the kitchen.

'Shall I help?'

'No need.'

He thought she would not understand Tamil traditions and things like that, so he had not told her about many such things. And if he ever told her about something like that, she did not even try to understand. In fact, she never paid any interest to anything that was Tamil. He wondered how to impress on her that the first tonsure, ear piercing and all should be done only in the kuladeivam temple.

'In our family, all auspicious ceremonies are celebrated only in the kuladeivam temple. Our wedding alone was not celebrated there. Your family did not agree to us getting married in the first place. On top of that, if I had said the wedding would be in my home town in my temple, your family would have said "no" point-blank. That is why I agreed to have the wedding in Delhi. My family was so angry with me for not getting married in the kuladeivam temple. It is a big mistake, do you know?'

'What is a mistake? Marrying me?' she snapped. He did not know what to say. He kept staring at the flame on the stove silently. He then looked at Varsha, who pretended to be busy with her cooking. She knew his eyes were on her, but not once did she meet his gaze.

'For six or seven generations, all our family weddings have been celebrated only in that temple.'

'Will the temple be big?'

'It will be only as big as a house. It is the place where Tiruneeru Sami was buried. We call that our temple.'

She took the pressure cooker off the stove and placed the vegetables on it to boil.

'So, the guy you speak about is not a god?'

'He was born as an ordinary mortal and grew up as such, but he did not live as one. He performed many miracles. He did not own anything and had no possessions, not even a plate to eat from. I have repeated this to you many times.'

'Oh.'

This word angered him. He thought she was perhaps mocking his kuladeivam.

'I thought it may be a big temple seeing how stubborn you are. Looks like it is just an ordinary man's cemetery, samadhi.' She then started chopping the vegetables, her actions and tone visibly indicating that going to the family temple was not so important or necessary to her.

'Just understand what I'm telling you. He was born in 1541 and that is about seven or eight generations earlier. He ran away from home while incredibly young and became a *siddha*. It is that person whom we worship as our kuladeivam.'

Varsha did not listen to these words at all. Instead, she loudly said, 'The baby is crying, go bring her.'

He picked up the crying child and returned to the kitchen. As soon as the child saw Varsha, she leapt towards her, but Varsha continued with her cooking. She did not take the child in her arms, nor did she seem to see the child coming to her. The child began to sneeze.

'Take her away to the hall.'

Annamalai carried the child to the hall. He drew open the curtains and amused the child by showing her the rows and rows of multi-storeyed buildings. The sneezing stopped only after some time. He drew back the curtains, returned to the sofa and switched on the TV. Varsha stopped her cooking midway and came and sat down to watch TV, deliberately avoiding looking at him. She also ignored the child who stretched out to reach her. He kept looking at her without blinking. Then in a tired voice, he said, 'You just don't know about the Siddhas.'

'Who are they? Do they do magic or cast spells?'

'No. Being a siddha is a way of life. It is divesting oneself of everything and owning nothing.' He then spoke about the Siddhas and their lives in detail. Varsha was not in the least impressed and did not even say something like, 'Really?' That did not upset him. 'A north Indian woman, she won't understand about Siddhas,' he thought.

'Are you determined that we must go to your kuladeivam temple?' she calmly asked, as though she was thinking of something.

'You wouldn't ask this question if you knew about Tiruneeru Sami fully.'

'The person you speak of is not a god, he was just an ordinary mortal.'

The words she spoke did not bother him, but the contempt in her tone when she said 'ordinary mortal' provoked his anger.

'This Swamiji you go to, calling him a great guru, do you know he owns properties worth several crores in India and abroad? He has branches in every country like a corporate entity. And properties everywhere. Can you call someone who rakes in money a god? Do you know anything about Tiruneeru Sami? He said, "Your own mind is the god, do as it says and don't go around calling a stone as god" and that "My tongue will not utter a lie." Siddhas are those who do not identify themselves by a name. It is the people who gave him the name Tiruneeru Sami. They may perform many miracles, but they go without leaving a trace, as they are the Siddhas.'

After listening to him with patience, she said kindly, 'I have work in the kitchen' and went to the kitchen at once. He was annoyed. He set the child on the floor and began to watch the TV, but he could not focus on it. He went near the windows, drew open the curtains and looked outside. As far as the eye could see, there were twenty- and thirty-storeyed buildings. He looked at each one of them but was unable to register anything. Varsha's words and actions burned inside him like live coal. He knew that if he continued the conversation, it would end in an argument. 'So be it,' he thought and rushed to the kitchen and spoke with the same urgency, 'Tiruneeru Sami is not some ordinary mortal like you think. The villagers challenged him saying if he is God, he must cook in an unburnt clay pot.'

Before he completed his words, Varsha butted in, 'He cooked in it, right?' He nodded. Suddenly he felt an urge to snub her.

'When the river was filled with water, the villagers asked him to walk across and . . .'

'. . . he did it, he crossed the river, right? I have heard this story many times.' She laughed.

'Not like you think. He walked on water like a light wooden piece floats and returned. It was then the villagers believed he was a divine person capable of miracles and began to worship him.'

'Let us not forget that both of us are scientists working in AIIMS.'

Her words and demeanour irritated him. *How do I make her understand?* He then saw the child crawling towards him and lifted her.

'How long will you take to finish work?'

'Ten minutes.' When she saw the child leaping towards her, she said, 'Take her to the hall, I'll be there.'

He did not go away and instead, asked her if she thought what he said about Tiruneeru Sami was a lie. She did not say anything in reply as she was focused on her cooking. Without paying heed to that, he said, 'That is not an ordinary temple. A two-headed snake is always found near the temple. No one is scared of it, nor do they hit it. They say that it is really Tiruneeru Sami who comes as the snake. The sounds of a bell ringing and the *udukkai** drum is heard at night. They say that the *sapthakannis,* the seven virgins, and the attendant deities dance around the temple. They have dug a well in the spot where Sami used to bathe when he was alive. It is 300–400 years old. Even in the height of summer or during the driest droughts, the well is without water. Anyone who goes to the temple steps inside only after drawing water from the well and bathing with it. The water in the well is as sweet as tender coconut water.'

Varsha was quietly doing her chores till Annamalai stopped speaking and then said, 'I have work to do.'

She began to wash the vessels. He got angry but spoke calmly without showing his anger, 'If you visit the temple, you'll know that all that I say is true.'

She replied in the end as though throwing a challenge, 'Even old grannies do not tell such nice stories.'

Her tone was arrogant and implacable, but he did not mind it. He wanted her to understand him.

'If you are sceptical, please read the book about Tiruneeru Sami that is on my bookshelf. How many times have I asked you to read those books? You never do what I say.'

---

* A small two-headed hourglass drum.

'Do I know Tamil?'

'A Tamil girl would have understood what I said by now.'

'Then you should have loved and married a Tamil girl . . . always talking about Tamil girls,' she shouted sternly.

'Just the mention of Tamil girls annoys northie girls,' he said in Tamil.

'What did you say?'

'Nothing.'

He walked to the hall carrying the child.

'I talk in Tamil about so many good things, but her deaf ear will not hear it and she will not understand what I said. But I just have to criticize her in Tamil, that she will understand,' he continued in Tamil in a very low voice. But somehow, she heard it and hastened towards him.

'You are criticizing me in Tamil, no?' she asked him angrily. But he did not get provoked and just laughed.

'You don't understand anything good that I say in Tamil but how do you understand clearly only when I criticize you?'

'I can guess just by looking at your darkened face.' She gritted her teeth.

'Why are you getting angry for a small matter? Come, sit down.' He grasped her arm and made her sit near him.

'You may say or do whatever you please, I will not make the trip to that temple.'

'Tickets have been bought. Can't change that now.'

'Will anyone go all that distance for a tonsure?'

'Don't talk nonsense.'

'I won't come. You may go, I won't stop you.'

'One must go with the family . . . that is the custom.'

'Leave me out of it.' She picked up the child and went to the bedroom. He followed her to appease her and make her agree. After he explained to her again the importance of going to the kuladeivam temple, she appeared as if she would consider it.

'See if we can do it online.'

'You are saying something stupid.'

'The Indians who live in USA do the *thithi* and other ceremonies online only.'

'Saris are bought online. They order beer, brandy, biryani, etc. online. Is going to the kuladeivam like that? If we continue like this, we will only end up fighting. Better to ask your mother to come and I will explain it to her.'

'You ask me to come to Tirupati, I will. But I won't ever come to the temple of that shit sami.'

'Shit sami, you said?' Without thinking, he slapped her cheek and regretted it at once.

'What did you do?' she asked repeatedly. She wept, called her mother and asked her to come at once. The child started crying because Varsha was crying. Annamalai got up and went to the hall. At once, she shut the bedroom door.

He was both confused and angry. It was four years now since he had married Varsha and for the first time, he wondered if his decision was right. He had gone to Delhi to do his PhD after completing his MSc in chemistry. It was there that he met Varsha, who was also doing her PhD. They became friends and it matured into something closer. They decided to get married only after they got jobs in AIIMS. Once that happened, they broached the matter to their families. It was her family which was more against it and objected. His family was doubtful if a north Indian girl would suit them, but the only condition they had imposed was that the wedding be performed in the family temple. Her family agreed to the marriage only because she was stubborn.

Now, their son was two years old, and their daughter was just a year old. Ever since they had gotten married, they had never had any big misunderstandings. Until today, he had not scolded her even once or even frowned at her. He had never done anything contrary to her preferences as she was the one who would argue more and insist that her wishes be followed. She would always insist that her way was right. It was just not in her nature to adjust to anyone. As he was repeatedly asking himself why he slapped her, the bell rang. When he opened the door, he was met with Varsha's mother Navaneeta Pande . . . an angry figure. She hastened to the bedroom and shut the door at once.

Annamalai was on the sofa watching TV, but his mind was filled with confused thoughts. He thought of his family and Varsha's. Navaneeta came out soon after talking to her daughter and sat on the sofa opposite him.

'I have lost all respect for you. It is disgusting. If you give Rs 50, the barber will do this job. Why fight over this? Tell me why you hit her,' she sputtered angrily and loudly.

'The first tonsure cannot be done in a barber's shop.'

'If it must be done in a temple, there are so many temples here, aren't they? We only need to go to one of those and get it done, no?' Her anger was increasing with no signs of cooling down.

'Can't be done in any other temple.'

'So, you must go *that* far, is it?'

'Yes, we must.'

'This is madness. You are living in some other times,' she said loudly.

'I thought you'd understand, being an older person.'

'It seems the place that you are talking about is not a temple at all, but the place where some person died.'

'Not some person . . . our ancestor.'

'He can be anyone, I don't care. Will anyone do an auspicious ceremony at some burial place?' She sounded harsh.

'You don't seem to know the customs of Tamil Nadu.'

'Because of your stubbornness, both of you must take leave from work and go on a tiring trip for four days. Will the children be able to stand it? The rainy season is not over yet in Delhi. If they fall sick because of a change in season, what then?' Her tone was peremptory.

'Nothing will happen.'

'How can you say that?'

'Tiruneeru Sami will take care of it.'

'Who is he?'

'Our family deity, kuladeivam.'

'Is there a god like that?' She laughed, full of contempt and disdain. Insolence was written large on her face.

'Don't laugh.'

Navaneeta's face changed when she heard Annamalai's tone. In these four years, he had never spoken to her so harshly. She was surprised when she saw him angry.

'I just laughed, sorry, I was not making fun.'

Ignoring her words, he said firmly, 'I will have my children's tonsure ceremony done in my kuladeivam temple.'

'Please think about it. There are so many temples here.' Navaneeta's voice did not have the earlier harshness. She looked at the TV, not wanting to look at him directly, but he looked straight at her.

'It has been decided, no room for changing my mind.'

Varsha then came out of the bedroom.

'If I don't come, what will you do?'

'My children and I will go.'

'The little one is only one year old. You'll take her too?'

'Definitely.'

'I won't come, nor will I send the children,' Varsha said conclusively.

His reply came like a slap.

'I'll divorce you and take them.'

Neither Varsha nor Navaneeta expected that he would use that word at the first stroke—they were both shocked and furious. Varsha kept looking at him without blinking. Navaneeta looked at the TV and all around, wanting to lighten the mood.

'Are you sure?' Varsha asked.

In a flash, he answered, 'Sure.'

His assertion shocked them more. They expected him to say that it was a slip of the tongue and that he did not mean it. But he did not say so. He spoke calmly, firmly, without any haste or agitation, which annoyed them more.

'Let us see that too.' Varsha's cheeks and lips trembled.

'Did you get married to my daughter only to divorce her?'

'No.'

'Then why did you say that?'

Annamalai sat calmly without saying anything. Varsha felt irritated by just looking at him. *He not only hit me but also said he would divorce me, and that too, in front of my mother*. Her anger flowed as tears. Seeing her, Navaneeta was also moved to tears, which infuriated Varsha uncontrollably.

'If I don't come to the temple of your choice, you will divorce me. But tell me how many times have I asked you to come to the Hanuman temple on our way? Have you come even once?'

'Until now, I have never gone to any temple except my family temple.'

'Is your god bigger than Hanuman?'

'Among gods, is there a big and small god?'

'Definitely, there is.'

'Then my family god is the big one. Why? Because he is the one who said, "Divinity is in you and your mind. There is no other god but you and your mind." Once some people asked him to visit the Tiruchendur temple. He refused saying that the god there is himself and he is that God, and why should he fall at his own feet? He also said that only men worship men.'

'It is unbelievable what you say. Just some story.'

'If what I say is just a story, then the Hanuman you worship is also a story. So are Rama and Sita . . . tales spun by Kamban and Valmiki.'

'Nooo, nooo,' Varsha shouted, gesturing as if to seek pardon for this sacrilege, and said, 'Jai Hanuman.' Navaneeta cast a look of burning rage at him.

'You can abuse human beings, not gods.'

'I am not abusing. Rama and Hanuman are creations of Valmiki in the north and Kamban in Tamil

Nadu. For both of them, Rama was not a god but just an ordinary character.'

'Don't say things like that,' Varsha and Navaneeta shouted at the same time.

He stopped talking. He sat there not wanting to look at these two women. They glared at him as though they could burn him to ashes.

'I am seeing a new Annamalai only today,' Navaneeta said, 'They say one must not trust a quiet person. That is true. Usually in Delhi, the impression is that all *Madrasis* are like mild-mannered clerks. I can see now that it is false.'

Varsha and Navaneeta looked pinched. Varsha made faces as though she was going to puke.

'What is our baby's name?' She wanted to needle him.

He looked as if it didn't matter to him if they frowned or grimaced.

'Tiruneeru Sami's mother's name is Unnamalai. Actually, it is the proper thing to name the child that. But because we are in Delhi, that name will not work. My mother's name is Umaiyal. That is another name for Unnamalai. So that will be my daughter's name.'

'Couldn't you find any other name in this whole wide world?' Navaneeta jeered.

'That is the name of my choice.'

'I detest it,' Varsha said.

'Then give your parents' names or your grandparents'. I won't stop you.'

'I prefer a modern name. Actually, I don't even like your name.' Varsha grimaced.

'I don't care. Because Tiruneeru Sami's name is Annamalai. In every home, not only in my town but even in surrounding places, there will be an Annamalai. In some homes, there may even be three Annamalais—Chinna Annamalai, Periya Annamalai and Nadu Annamalai—small, big and middle.'

'Is that name only for the men in your town or even for the women?' Navaneeta asked insolently. He was indifferent to that and replied with no change in his voice or face.

'Women will be named Unnamalai.'

'In every home?' Navaneeta was surprised.

'There will not be any family without at least one Unnamalai.'

'I think I must come to your place just to ascertain this,' Navaneeta said.

'Anyone in your town can give any name to anybody. I refuse to give my children such old-fashioned names and that too Tamil names . . . never. Even in your place, children now have north Indian names.'

He neither opened his mouth nor looked at Varsha or Navaneeta.

'Finish the rites in some temple here itself. I agree it is not good that the tonsure and naming of the children are still not performed,' Navaneeta said, appearing to agree with him. Annamalai frowned, indicating his disagreement.

'We should have gone there during the boy's first year itself. I thought let the second child turn one year old. That is why I waited. She is a year old now. I bought the tickets only because I felt it should not be delayed any longer. But Varsha got upset.'

Navaneeta and Varsha thought he had lost his senses. *He repeats the same thing. He insists he is right. What kind of fellow is he?* they wondered. As though a thought had suddenly struck her, Varsha asked, 'Is this why you kept quiet when I asked you to suggest a name when our son was born?'

'Yes. I have also explained it several times and you know it.'

'Don't strain yourself going all that way. See that it is done here itself,' Navaneeta Pande said.

'I will go to my place and do it only there. Nowhere else.'

'Behave like an educated person, you have studied so much,' Navaneeta said, and his face changed.

'My subject was not about persons or their lives, but facts and data. That is the problem.'

'My mother meant something else.' Varsha frowned at him, but he did not look at her.

'I know, Varsha. I don't mind if you both think I am a fool. My decision will not change.'

'What more can I say?' Navaneeta was fed up. Then in a mocking tone, she said, 'Don't name your son after your god.'

'The proper thing is to name him Annaamalai. But we can't do that since that is my name. One option is Arunachalam, but you won't agree, so his name will be Arunachaleswar. Varsha, I'll agree with anything you say, and do as you say, but let me have my way in this matter of the children, please,' he pleaded.

'I will not call them by those names you have chosen,' Varsha said stubbornly, turning her head away.

'As you wish,' he said bluntly.

'Only I will name them. I'll call them only by that name.'

'You give them any name you like and call them what you will. But the names I have chosen alone will be on the certificate.'

'What kind of names are they . . . the ones you say?' Navaneeta asked.

'They are good names; rarely will you get names like that.'

'Annamalai . . . Unnamalai . . . what kind of shit names are they?'

Insane with rage, he slapped her on the cheek. 'If you repeat this word again, you will not be alive. It is because we must not forget our ancestors that we pray to them and name our children after them, understand?' he yelled at her.

He had not only slapped her twice that day but also in front of her mother. Her anger knew no limits.

Avoiding her mother's eyes, she ran to her bedroom and locked herself in.

'O! You'll slap my daughter right in front of me, is it? She was weeping, did you see? This is the great Tamil Nadu custom, is it?' She raved for a while. But Annamalai did not say anything in response. She went and knocked on the door. Varsha opened the door only after Navaneeta had knocked multiple times.

'Come, let us go home.' Navaneeta grasped Varsha's hand. Just then the sleeping child began to cry. Varsha went back to pick her up and Navaneeta followed her. The next moment, the bedroom door slammed shut. Annamalai kept staring at the closed door.

He then looked out of the window—all the dwelling apartments that he saw appeared to him like mere buildings. So many buildings. Then he saw the Bihari hand-rickshaw men standing at the corner of the apartment complex. Nothing registered in his mind. His eyes saw the buildings, but his mind was only seeing the Tiruneeru Sami temple. So many memories moved past in his mind, his father carrying him on his shoulders, walking with akka, his elder sister, holding her hand, going with the townspeople in the bullock cart, praying at the temple before tenth board exams with the hall ticket, praying there with the hall-ticket before the twelfth grade exams, before every exam when studying BSc and MSc, placing the PhD application at the temple and praying, when he got the job and the appointment order and then also praying there with the wedding invitation. Not only his family, but the whole town believed that all the good things that happened to him were because of Tiruneeru Sami. Not once had he failed in any exam he had written. Every time he went to the temple, he would sit there looking at the *spatikalingam*, the crystal *lingam*. At those moments it would feel as if he was free from his body and his life. He felt a deep resentment against Varsha. He felt a hatred for Delhi. He thought it was a big mistake coming to Delhi to study, getting a job there, falling in love with Varsha and marrying her . . . all a big mistake.

'If you take a job in the north, you'll stop coming here. Can't you get any job here for your qualification?' He remembered his akka, Unnamalai, asking him sadly. He also remembered her crying when he told her he was going to marry Varsha.

'If you marry a north Indian, how can you come here? You can't come here frequently to see our relatives and our people. I have only one brother. If I let you also go with a north Indian girl, what is left for me on this soil . . . in this place?' She had pleaded so much and had tried to persuade him to choose a girl from Tamil Nadu. He had refused to listen to her or anything that she or his people said. He now wondered what stopped him from listening to them.

After much pleading, his akka finally said, 'You may forget anything or anyone, but never forget our family deity, our kuladeivam. Among everyone in and around this place, you are the one who has studied so much and got such a big job. All this is because of our kuladeivam's grace. Never ever forget that.' She went away crying. As he recalled that, his eyes became wet as well. If his parents had been alive, even if they had agreed to him taking up a job in Delhi, they would have refused point-blank him marrying Varsha. He thought it was better that they were not alive to hear Varsha say she would not come to the Tiruneeru Sami temple. *Why is she so stubborn? She had never been so stubborn or spoken so arrogantly before.*

The more he thought of her, the more confused he became and the angrier he got. He turned away to calm himself. On his east, he saw the Ring Road winding to Sri Aurobindo Marg. He saw cars scurrying like ants.

The calling bell rang. Wondering who it could be, he opened the door. It was Varsha's elder brother, Alok Pande.

'Please come in.'

Alok merely smiled—it was a lifeless smile. He came in and they sat opposite each other. They heard Varsha's mother shouting.

'I told you right at the beginning that marrying a Madrasi won't work. Did you listen to me? You threw a tantrum, you cried, you said you would die. Now see what happened. He slapped you right in front of me. What are you going to do now? You did not like any of the Delhi boys. Now you are being beaten black and blue.' When he heard both of them crying inside, Alok got agitated.

'What happened?'

Annamalai said nothing. Alok sprang up and knocked on the door. It was Navaneeta who opened it. As soon as she saw Alok, she started crying. He went in and the door was shut yet again. Navaneeta could be clearly heard scolding Varsha for falling in love with Annamalai and marrying him. Annamalai stood outside, calmly listening to all the abuses.

In a few minutes, Alok came out and sat in the hall. Annamalai stood in front of the window looking at the buildings. Alok called his name and Annamalai came and sat in front of him.

'Couldn't you have told me a word about all this?' the older man asked.

Annamalai did not utter a word.

'I never dreamt you'd lose your temper.'

Even then Annamalai did not say anything.

'We knew nothing about you, your town, your family, your place, not even your language. We gave our girl because of your character—it made us trust you. It was not even because of your qualifications.'

He said nothing.

'Varsha is weeping and so is my mother. It breaks my heart to see them, Annamalai.' Alok's face changed and his voice too.

'It is a small matter, leave it.' Annamalai sounded bitter.

Varsha came out of the bedroom and screamed, 'What is a small matter?'

She then vented all her grievances against him in the last four years. He did not say a word. As if Varsha screaming was not enough, Navaneeta added her bit.

'Let me speak, please be quiet,' Alok said, but neither Varsha nor Navaneeta paid any heed to him. He waited patiently for a while and then he shouted, 'If you are going to yell like this, why did you call me?' Only after that did the two women quieten.

'I'll deal with this, you both go inside.'

Alok calmed down only after he sent them inside the bedroom.

'What happened?' Alok asked.

'I bought tickets to go to our kuladeivam temple to do the tonsure for the children. She is raising a ruckus and refusing to come. They are provoking me to violence and taking me for a fool.'

Hearing this, Varsha came out of the bedroom and asked, 'So will you slap me twice and say you will divorce me just because I said I won't come?'

'I did not slap you or say I'll divorce you just for refusing to come to the temple. You must not twist facts.'

'Then why did you hit me? Or say those words?' Her words came like a slap.

'You insulted my kuladeivam, you called him a shit god and said his name is a shit name. That's why.'

'I'll repeat it. Will you hit me?'

'Certainly.'

'Is that so?' Varsha shouted and Navaneeta, who had entered the hall, shouted louder.

'Why are you getting angry and shouting?' Alok asked. The two women were not prepared to listen to him, but he attempted to calm them.

'You have never gone to Tamil Nadu. Let this be an excuse to visit.'

'Did you come all the way to say this? Have you gone mad?' Varsha shouted at him.

'First, stop screaming. He was wrong to have slapped you and also to have said he would divorce you. But you are also wrong to refuse to go with him.'

'Then you go with him.' She was stubborn.

'Please try to understand me.'

'You go with him,' Varsha said, weeping.

'He is only saying he wants to go to the temple. What's wrong with that?'

'What are you saying? Have you lost your senses?' Navaneeta asked and before he could reply, she continued, 'I realize now that it is possible to earn a good name and also to deceive others just by being silent. For the first time I am hearing that, even in 2016, a person will insist on travelling 2000–3000 km just for a child's tonsure.'

Alok spoke. Varsha spoke. Navaneeta spoke. Annamalai did not open his mouth to utter one word. It was only after all three forced him to say if there was another option, that he spoke slowly.

'In Tamil Nadu, no woman will interrogate her son-in-law sitting like this on the sofa, with one leg over the other.'

Not only Alok Pande and Varsha but even Navaneeta did not know how to respond to this.

'Your every word is toxic,' Navaneeta said and went to the bedroom. The fact that Navaneeta was upset enraged Varsha more than ever.

'Forever, this bragging about Tamil Nadu. You don't know how to respect others. Is slapping your wife shamelessly part of the proud culture of Tamils? If the neighbouring flat residents knew you hit me, what would they think?' Varsha darted questions one after another. In the end, she said, 'Who are you to divorce me? I'll divorce you myself.' She began to rummage for some papers.

'You go inside now. I'll talk to him.' Alok compelled her to go in and then returned to his seat.

'What is your plan?' he asked Annamalai calmly.

He clearly detailed his four-day plan—going to Chennai by flight, from there by train, taking a cab from the railway station, picking up his sister and going with her to the temple, finishing the rituals, going straight back to the station, back to Chennai and then to Delhi again. Alok listened to all this patiently.

'Is your family deity Krishna or Siva?'

'Neither.'

'Will the temple be like the Chidambaram Nataraja temple or Madurai Meenakshi temple?'

'Not like them.'

'Oh.' He did not sound pleased or mocking. All of a sudden, he asked if Annamalai had a photo of the deity.

'In those days, no one took photos or videos.' Annamalai attempted a smile. His face, which had become tight and tense when Varsha and Navaneeta were screaming, was only now relaxing a little.

'Do you have any sloka he wrote, songs or any book or predictions?'

Annamalai twisted his lips indicating a no.

'Then how do you say he is god?' He sounded tired.

'It is because he had nothing like that, that he is god.'

'Any branch anywhere else?'

'To have branches in every other place—is this a company, bank, textile shop or restaurant?'

Alok frowned on hearing this and thought he must bring the conversation to an end. Yet, he continued with a question.

'Is there anything like a *gurukulam*, trust, *math*, yoga centre or a *dhyana mandapam*?'

'Nothing of that sort. He said, "We are our own burden, the mind alone is our enemy, kill the mind and still the mind. The mind is a devil, kill it." He lived his life like that. He was not interested in things like what you mention.'

'Has he foretold the future?'

Annamalai was fed up. He was even irritated with Alok for asking such a question. If Varsha and

Navaneeta troubled him in one way, this one was causing another kind of trouble. But for the first time, he wondered why Tiruneeru Sami never did any of these things. Still, he repeated Tiruneeru Sami's words.

'*Speak less, speak less, eat less, eat less, just be, just be*. These were his words.'

'Oh.'

'He foretold his day of death.'

'Really?' Alok was surprised.

'He said, "My task here is complete, I have received the call to return, my karma is over, I will be leaving this body on the full moon day, the star Uttarattadhi and month of Purattasi, get the burial pit ready." Exactly on that day, he descended the pit and covered the pit himself with a huge rock. They lifted the stone a year later and found no rotting remains, no skeleton, nothing but a crystal lingam. They installed it and built a temple. It is that which I call Tiruneeru Sami.'

'What you say is amazing.'

'The Siddhas of Tamil Nadu are miraculous, sir. There have been people like this right from the seventh century. The siddha tradition starts from Tirumoolar. They wrote that "those who know themselves will forget the self, it is those who do not know themselves who will project themselves."'

'Listening to what you say surprises me, and also frightens me that you will become a siddha yourself.' Alok laughed out loud, but Annamalai did not feel like laughing. He just sat quietly. Alok looked at his face keenly and started to say something but stopped. Then he went to the refrigerator and drank some water from a bottle. He returned to sit down and said in a teasing voice, 'So tell me, *siddhar*.'

'My mind is not ready to become a siddhar. It is just like a rat hole. To become a siddha, the mind should be more expansive than the sea. To be aware that the mind is not the sea, one must have that recognition and wisdom. That will not happen for everyone. "O! Foolish mind, though you are in the stream, you cannot see the shore, life is false, death is truth." This is the tradition of the Siddhas. The inscription on our temple entrance says, "Know yourself and be free of sorrow."'

'Will the temple be very big?'

'No.'

'Are there any disciples?'

'In a siddha's life, there is no guru, no *sishya*. There is no giving and no taking. He does not study the Vedas, he does not go on pilgrimages, he does not do meditation and he does not set up maths, *adheenams* or gurukulams. He does not want to become a *mathadhipathi*, *adheenakartha*, guru or a spiritual teacher. He does not receive initiation from a guru. He does not give initiation to anyone, does not become a renunciate or wear ochre robes. They believe that getting involved with "food", which means all things material, is the root of the misery of *samsara*. Their life is free of attachment, like the ripe tamarind fruit, where the tamarind stays detached from the shell.'

'All this is new to me.'

'Tiruneeru Sami is not the real name of my *kuladeivam*. His name is Annamalai. The people believed that seeing a liberated person liberates one from all curses. So, *they* called him sami, *they* called him a siddhar. Never ever did he declare himself to be a sami or a siddhar. He said that both your heaven and your hell are inside you alone. The Siddhas are those who did not even utter their own names. Their names and their identities are derived only from their deeds and their lives. Even their names were given to them by the people. And also, their identities. There are so many even now, like Thaliayatti siddhar, Kaarai siddhar, Suraikkai siddhar, Madhagu siddhar, Aathusami, Theepettisami, Madi sami and so on. In the olden days, there were many Siddhas like Pambaatti siddhar, Sivavakyar, Pathiragiri and so on and none of these names were given to them by themselves. If you don't believe me, go to Tamil Nadu and visit places like Chaduragiri Hill, Mahendra Hill, Surli Hill, Kolli Hill, Nambi Hill and Pacha Hill. You can see there have been many Siddhas. In fact, there is a rock called Sanyasi Rock.'

'As I said, this is all new to me.'

'Sir, the life that we know is different from the life that we seek. The life of a true siddha was one where the ego was killed, where they erased their own footprints and thought even their own shadows were a burden. They celebrated death. They wanted death, which was their only wish.'

Alok looked at Annamalai curiously—his face and expression had a newness, and his voice and speech were not rushed. He could not believe that Annamalai was talking non-stop like a history professor. Alok had never seen him talk much and he had always spoken as little as possible to Varsha's people. He would just answer the questions asked and that too, not loudly or sharply. He never said anything on his own and would not even openly say 'yes' to anything, he would just nod indicating a 'yes'. If a matter was under discussion, he never argued that his view alone was correct. That was how he spoke to Varsha too, not just the others. It was only because of his good nature that Varsha's family had agreed to the marriage, though he was from Tamil Nadu and dark-complexioned. He always addressed Alok and his father, as 'sir'. But now Annamalai had slapped Varsha and that too, in front of their mother, and declared that he would divorce Varsha. Alok thought of all this one after another and forgot that he had been called by Varsha and Navaneeta to scold Annamalai, correct him and tell him that going to the kuladeivam temple was a no-no.

'What did your god eat?'

'It seems people who came to see him offered fruits, but he never even looked at them. Crows, vultures, sparrows and other birds would come and peck at

them. It seems flies and ants never came near those
fruits. And they never rotted, even after many days.'

'Really?'

'He had mastered the eight *siddhis*, magical powers,
yoga siddhi and many such things. They said that he
was under a banyan tree and in the Muruga temple in
Tiruchendur, all at the same time, and was capable of
transmigrating. It is because he performed such siddha
acts that he is called a siddha.'

'People must have come to ascetics like this, asking
for this and that, praying that this should happen or
that. What did he do for them?'

'To them, he would say, "Go round this arasa
tree repeating, 'The sea is not mine, the wind is not
mine, the earth is not mine, nor is the mountain.
The water is not mine nor the soil. This village is
not mine nor is the world. This body is not mine nor
is this life.'" Hearing this, the people said, "What
kind of a crack, sami, this is?" So, he was also called
Cracksami. People prayed to him that their business
should improve, that they should construct a house,
they should start an industry and so on. His reply
was, "Your sami is full, then why do you need all this
nonsense?" People did not understand him. "What
are you saying, sami?" He said, "I am referring to
your belly. That is full and not empty. Then what
else do you want? The biggest deity in this world is
our belly. When that is satisfied, why do you need
anything else? The fire of hunger alone is our biggest

burden. If you are able to forget hunger, the rest is forgotten and all sorrows will cease." Even though he spoke like this and they called him Cracksami, the crowds continued to be drawn to him. When people came and prayed that they were childless and they wanted a child, his reply was, "Catch the wind and give it to me, catch the brightness and give it to me, I'll give you what you pray for," and he sent them off. If his relatives and acquaintances came, he asked, "Why are you coming to me like a bull stamping on a fallen man? This is a cart without an axle, do not load your burden on this." That was him.'

The more Alok heard what Annamalai said, the more curious he became to know about Tiruneeru Sami. But he was also feeling very hungry. *Varsha and Navaneeta are talking inside the bedroom. Here, Annamalai is going on non-stop.* He wondered if it would be out of place to mention lunch at this moment and considered going home. But he was not sure if it would be proper to do that when this man was talking about something so intensely. He also wanted to know more about Tiruneeru Sami.

'Did your sami become like this when he was young? Or did he get married and then renounce the world?'

'They seem to have forced him to get married. "You must not tie two elephants to one pillar. The entire world lives only for their descendants and children. I do not want that life," was his reply. But his family was adamant that he should get married, so he ran away from home and never returned.'

'Where was his town?'

'Same as mine. Aanpillaipirandan is the name of the town, which means a male child was born.'

'Strange name.' Alok laughed in spite of his hunger.

'You will laugh more if you hear the name of the place where he spent his days and died.'

'What is that?'

'Vazhvangi, meaning life well-lived.'

Alok said that it was a splendid name.

'Annie Besant came to our temple and built an arch with her own money. Vivekananda stayed there for five days and meditated. Eyden, who was our district collector, visited it. Bhagawan Ramana came and paid his respects. Sir, Bharati, the modern poet of Tamil Nadu, wrote about him as the light that came to drive away the dirt in our heart and the diseases in our body.'

Alok Pande's amazement peaked when he heard this.

'Just one minute,' he said and ran to the bedroom, where he told Varsha and Navaneeta breathlessly about all the visitors to the temple. Varsha listened to his outburst calmly and patiently and then deflated his excitement.

'A story without a head or tail.'

'I really believe Annamalai will not lie to us.'

'He will not tell lies, but he will tell us stories.' Her words reflected clearly that she was angry with

Annamalai. So Alok decided not to talk about this to her. He turned to his mother.

'It is getting late, shouldn't we have lunch?'

'He has slapped my daughter in front of me. You haven't asked him about it, you have not warned him and instead, you are repeating his stories to me. Aren't you ashamed?' Navaneeta lashed out.

It was obvious that if Varsha was 100 per cent furious with Annamalai, Navaneeta was ten times more furious. Alok went back to his seat in the hall without saying a word. He wondered if what Annamalai had told him were lies, fables or just some oral stories. 'Asking him directly would be rude,' he thought, but he still could not control himself from clearing his doubt.

'Is it true . . . all that you are telling me?'

Annamalai went to the bookshelf without replying, pulled out twenty or thirty books and placed them on the sofa. He picked out one book from them and showed the pictures to Alok. They were the photographs of Vivekananda, Ramana, Bharati, K.B. Sundarambal, Annie Besant and Eyden. Alok saw them one by one and said, 'Great!'.

'Shall I give you another book containing photos of those who have visited Tiruneeru Sami temple? Are you willing to see it? All the politicians and VIPs of Tamil Nadu will be there.' Then he picked out another book and showed Alok some more photographs.

'I have hundreds of stories about Tiruneeru Sami. You will refuse to believe them.'

'I will believe them,' Alok assured firmly. Then he took the two books that Annamalai had shown him and eagerly showed Varsha the pictures of Vivekananda, Annie Besant and Eyden.

'See this . . . and this . . . and this!' he gushed.

Varsha looked at him and asked calmly, 'Have you also become mad like him, *bhaiyya*?'

'Both of you just see these.' He gave them the books and returned to Annamalai.

'It is truly amazing.'

'These are not all. The miracles he performed are really the main things. He lit a lamp filled with water. He turned a copper plate into gold. He cooked food in an unburnt pot. When sick people came to him to be cured, he put a pinch of sand in their mouth and it turned to sacred ash. It seems like stomach aches, fevers, headaches and more would vanish. It is because of him that the town and the environs are well-known. Otherwise, what is there to speak of them? It would just have had the name Vazhvangi. Even the smallest of details about him have now become legends and history. Thus, the legend about Tiruneeru Sami has grown over generations and has not died. In Vazhvangi, there is no liquor shop, police station or cinema hall. No one in that town has ever stepped into a police station or court. Whenever there is a problem, the people from every caste in the town will assemble, discuss and arrive at a solution and declare it. No one till now has violated that.'

'The more I listen to you, the more amazed I am.'

'The ones who have moved away from the commonplace life and transformed, turn into legends. The rest of us who cannot think beyond *my* house, *my* room, *my* computer, *my* mobile phone and live around *me-my-mine* . . . we cannot achieve anything. At the entrance of the temple, these words are written, "*Thavanseyvaar tham karumam seyvaar matrallaar avanseyvaar aasaiyutpattu*" sir.'

'What does that mean?'

Annamalai explained the meaning in Hindi. (Those who renounce and perform austerities are the ones who fulfil their duties, all the others get trapped in desires and destroy themselves.)

'You speak Hindi better than us,' Alok said, laughing. 'The gold offered in Tirupati temple is kept in a deposit box. Is there anything like that in your temple? How much will the annual income be?'

'There are no boxes to drop your offerings in this temple.'

'What? How can a temple survive without money?'

'Had he been alive, he would not have permitted this temple to be built. He would have said, "This air around us is God and so are the earth, the sky, the water and the sun. Are you trying to put them inside a temple?" The land on which the temple stands today was given as a gift by a king in those days.'

'Really?'

'That is a long story.' Annamalai sounded tired.

Alok compelled him to narrate that story.

'The king who ruled over our place in those days suddenly developed a severe stomach ache. They tried several treatments but to no avail. Someone then told the king about the sami and the king ordered his attendants to bring him. They approached Tiruneeru Sami and requested him to come with them. He said, "It is the thirsty calf that should come to the pond, the pond will not go where the calf is," and sent them away.'

'Beautiful. Then?' Alok was like a child listening to a story.

'The messengers went back and reported to the king. The enraged king said, "Tie the fellow and bring him." Ten or twenty men came to call the sami but he refused. They tried to lift him and carry him. He laughed at them. "Who dares to lift the air? Who can lift the sea and the mountain and this light?" The messengers reported this to the king. He was so furious that he wanted to order that the sami's head be severed, but he also wanted a cure for his stomach ache. So, he relented and came to see the sami in person. Tiruneeru Sami applied a pinch of sand on the king's stomach and in the next moment, the pain vanished. "You have cured me of the incurable stomach ache. Ask me for anything and I will give it to you," the king said. The sami asked the king, "How will you reward the air, the sea, the sky, Mother Earth, the light and the sun? Go away." The king replied, "It is your nature

to refuse, but to go away without giving is not mine."
Sami then said, "Look up. Pattinathaar, Sivavakkiyar,
Pathiragiriyaar and Pambaatti siddhar are travelling
across the sky. I need to talk to them, you move
away." Saying this, he started saying namaste looking
at the sky. The king said, "The ascetic and the lunatic
will not listen to anyone. It does not befit me to go
away without rewarding you. I am now going to whip
this horse. It will start galloping, get tired after some
time and slow down to a trot. The land from here till
there, I will donate to you." The king then whipped the
horse. It ran and ran till it got tired and the place where
it stopped running was marked. The king signed a deed
in which all the land from the arasa tree to that spot
was endowed to Tiruneeru Sami and then went away.'

'Astonishing. Is that place still in use?'

'Yes.'

'Who built the temple?'

'One Punnaivanam Chettiar said that sami came in
his dream and told him to build his temple, and it is he
who built the present temple.'

'Hasn't your family done anything?'

'No. They have worshipped there. That is all.'

'Who is that Chettiar?'

'He was a trader. In those days, when he had gone
overseas and conducted his business, it suffered huge
losses. One day after bathing in the river, he walked
past the arasa tree when Tiruneeru Sami was there.
Prodded by some impulse, he wept to him about the

loss. Sami gave him a handful of sand which turned into gold and with that, he started his business again and became a millionaire. Once he became rich, Punnaivanam Chettiar brought three or four bags filled with money and emptied them at Sami's feet. Sami asked him, "Why are you bringing this rubbish here? It is because of this that all the miseries of this world happen. Now even burnt embers are sold and encashed by this world. Take this away and throw it in the river." Because those were Sami's words, Chettiar emptied all that money in the river.'

'Miracle.' Alok was open-mouthed with wonder. 'I can't decide who is greater, the Sami or Chettiar . . . Now how do you know all this?'

'It is what was orally shared by the people who were with him, who knew him or had seen it in person. Then it became a tale and history. It is not just Chettiar, anyone who goes to the temple and pours his woes will be relieved of them. People who are unmarried or childless have their prayers answered.'

'Even now?'

'Yes, even now. You will find it hard to believe that the person who distributes the *tiruneeru*, the sacred ash, at the temple is a Muslim.'

'What?' Alok nearly jumped.

'Truly, sir. In those days, there was a man called Vethilaipettai Alauddin who had thirteen children. His business was selling vettilai or betel leaves. He had an extremely poor family and would go all over selling betel leaves. On one such trip, he had come and sat under the arasa tree's shade. There, he kept on staring at Sami and found himself telling him all his problems. Sami did not say a word but gave him a handful of sand and sent him away. From the next day onwards, Alauddin's business picked up. It grew so much that he began exporting to Sri Lanka, Kumbakonam seeval, Nagapattinam cheroot, Tanjore betel leaves, Tiruchendur chillukaruppatti (palm jaggery), Kodai road grapes, Malainadu plantains, pears, Cholavandaan betel leaves and more. He firmly believed that his prosperity was because of Sami and started coming to see Sami daily. After Sami died, it was he who came every full moon day and distributed tiruneeru. After him, his wife, Ayesha Biwi did it. Then their eldest son, Khaja Moideen did it. Then his son, Jamal Mohammed gave it. Now, it is being done by Raja Mohammed. The maximum crowd will come on the full moon of the month *Avani*, which will be from 15 August to 15 September. Even though my family is related to Tiruneeru Sami, we will receive the tiruneeru only from them.'

'How did this happen?'

'I don't know. But since those days, this is the practice.'

'Hasn't there been any quarrel?'

'For what?'

'Because Muslims are giving the tiruneeru.'

'To date, no one has objected.'

'Which god do those people worship?'

'Of course, Allah.'

'When did you last go to the temple?'

'Last year Avani.'

'Who gave tiruneeru then?'

'Of course, Raja Mohammed.'

'Has there never been even one instance when someone objected?'

'Is god there to create rifts and divisions between people?'

'Beautiful. Just wait here.' Alok went in and told his mother and sister about the Muslims and Tiruneeru Sami temple. His face was radiant with joy. Navaneeta looked at him and turned away, calling him an idiot.

'Story over and done. It is the same story I have been hearing for four years,' Varsha said derisively.

'Do you think it is just a story?'

'I think it is a fabricated story.' Varsha's face was red. Alok stood there, not knowing what to say. She then barked at him, 'Does their god say beat your wife and divorce her?'

Alok had to say something so he just told them, 'Have lunch, it is getting late,' and returned to Annamalai.

'I want to visit the temple once.'

'The actual tradition is the child will sit on the *mama,* the uncle's, lap when the head is tonsured, ears are pierced and the name is given. I did not tell you because you are north Indians. The entire expense is traditionally done by the mama and that is you.'

'Is that so? I'll do it. I'll keep the child on my lap while all that is done. I am happy just thinking of it. Buy the ticket,' Alok said. Then he looked at all the books scattered on the sofa and asked Annamalai if they were all written by his Sami.

'No. They are written by others about him.'

'Okay. Book the tickets. Now let us eat,' Alok hurried him and then told Varsha, 'Cool down. I will also come, let Amma come too. We will go together. I am bound to do all this.'

'Didn't he slap me before Amma and say he would divorce me and take the children with him? I will not come . . . even if I die,' Varsha said weeping.

Annamalai spoke in a calm and measured tone. 'Even if Tiruneeru Sami came in person and told me not to go, I will not listen. For my children, the tonsure, the ear-piercing and naming ceremonies will be done only in my kuladeivam temple.'

Samban, Son of Krishna—An Untold Tale

The Samban of this story is none other than the son born to Jambavati and Krishna. Harichandran suffered great agony because of Viswamitra's scheming. Duryodana and his brothers suffered and died because of the cunning Sakuni. This is the saga of Samban's suffering because of Narada's wily plot.

* * *

'When the sage Narada was perambulating the world, it suddenly occurred to him that he should meet Krishna. At once, he set off to Dwarka. He first went to see Vasudeva, the noblest of the Yadu clan and father of Krishna. Vasudeva was immensely delighted and accorded all hospitality and honours that were due to the great sage. Thereafter, Narada went to see Krishna who was living on the peak of the Raivata hill. Krishna ran to welcome Narada as he approached his palace and received him with all honours. Along with him, thousands of the Vrishni family bowed down before Narada. All the wives of Krishna and his son,

Pradyumna, fell at the sage's feet. Narada was delighted
by this warm reception. His eyes turned towards the
garden. He saw Samban, who had the effulgence of
a thousand suns, cavorting in a sensual sport with
women. 'Who is that?' he asked. Krishna replied that
it was his son Samban, born to Jambavati.

Narada spent many hours in Krishna's abode,
but Samban did not come to pay his respects. His
attention was focused on playing with the young men
and women. Narada saw that the hundreds of young
women in the garden only wanted to be with Samban
and join him in a sexual union.

Of all the sons of Krishna, Samban was the most
handsome. He possessed a matchless beauty with a
touch of the divine and glowed like the metal that is
hammered in a fire. His frame was golden and women
competed with one another to see him. Narada learnt
that the Yadava women loved Samban more than their
own lives and he got enraged that Samban had not
come to pay his obeisance to him even after so long.
He then made enquiries about Samban—everyone
had only good things to say of him and it seemed like
he had no faults at all. The sage's anger grew more
intense. Narada thought he must destroy Samban's
beauty, for women were attracted to it and it kept him
ensnared in that web of attraction. He thought about
what the best way would be to punish Samban for
ignoring him. If he found faults in him, no one would
accept them. Narada knew that Samban was virtuous,

noble and compassionate and that he never spoke ill of anyone. He wondered what would stoke the flame of jealousy in Krishna. He knew that his desire for women alone would do it as it was the women who ran towards him. So, he decided to execute a devious plot with the father and son that would make Samban fall at his feet.

He went to Krishna.

'A shadow of shame has fallen on your clan because of Jambavati's son, Samban.'

Krishna spoke of Samban's virtues and how well he conducted himself towards the elders. This only infuriated Narada.

'Your 16,000 wives are all caught in the spell of Samban's beauty and pining to unite with him.'

Krishna replied, opposing Narada for the first time.

'Except for Rukmini, Satyabama, Jambavati, Kalindi, Mitravinda Nagnajithi, Bhadra and Lakshmanaa, all the others were captured by me, brought here and then I married them. They are also bound to me. I will not believe this accusation.'

'Do you want me to produce proof of it?'

'Yes, give me proof.'

'I will produce it at the appropriate time,' Narada said and left Krishna's palace angrily.

Krishna thought about the matter deeply, but he could not find any fault in Samban. Soon after, he forgot all about it. But Narada, who was sly, cunning, vengeful and vile, did not forget it—his wrath against

Samban burned like fire inside him. He waited for the right time and when it came, he left for Dwarka again.

Samban was happily entertaining himself with women in the royal garden.

'Your father wants you to meet him in the Raivataka hill garden at once.'

This was the time when Krishna would be with his 16,000 wives and no one would venture to enter the place. So, Samban hesitated.

'Do you doubt my words?'

'No, you are the sage of all sages. How can the words that fall from you be false? I will go and meet my father as ordered by you.' He bowed down to Narada and went to Krishna's harem garden.

Ill omens welcomed him. He was perturbed, but he did not let that deter him and went on.

Krishna was there, unclothed and engaged in amorous sport with his wives. Seeing this, Samban felt embarrassed and tried to turn back, but many women who had been abducted, imprisoned and brought by Krishna, saw him. Captivated by his looks, they tried to lure him in by revealing their beauty. Krishna saw these women who were besotted with Samban and was angry.

'All of you, though married to me, strayed from the righteous path by behaving like this. You will be reborn as hunting hounds roaming the mountains and will get caught by bandits and tortured by them. In the other births, you will be born as ghouls.'

Then he turned to Samban, his anger still raging.

'And you! You came where you ought not to come. You committed an unspeakably evil act. May your beauty that enthrals your own mothers be destroyed at once! All these 1000 women shyly look down now because of your beauty. That beauty will be disfigured and from now on, the world will turn away from you in revulsion. The handsome frame that made women besotted, will change. It shall transform into a leprous body shunned by the world. The world will revile you. Just as seeds sown on this earth start to sprout, from this month, leprous sores will appear on your body,' Krishna cursed. Everything was over in a second, in a flash of lightning.

'I did not come on my own. It is only because the sage Narada told me that I came. I have not done any wrong. Why did you curse me so terribly?' Samban was weeping, beseeching and trembling. Rukmini, Satyabama and Jambavati were also weeping inconsolably. It was only when his temper cooled down that Krishna understood the whole truth. Grief for his son gripped him and his mind was changing when Narada appeared.

'Krishna, you are all-knowing and omniscient. Yet you cursed in haste, unconcerned that he is your son. That is because of your jealousy. It proves that even you cannot escape it. This is an opportunity for you to understand the female mind. Do you understand the truth now? Right before your eyes, your wives were attracted to another man and that too, your own son. You saw it and you cursed. Once before, you asked me for proof. I produced it. What are you going to do now? I know that Samban is innocent. You know it too. In spite of that, you cursed him. How are you going to release him from the curse? He must suffer the curse and he must undergo it. That is my wish.'

Krishna was speechless, immersed as he was in confusion.

'I am innocent. I am guilty of no sin. I have not committed any wrong. Why have I been punished so severely? Why did you curse me?' Samban asked. His words may have been aimed to clear Krishna's confusion. His heart was like molten lava. Rukmini, Satyabama and Jambavati fell at Krishna's and Narada's feet and pleaded, prayed and beseeched them to relieve Samban of the effect of the curse. Narada then smiled at Krishna cunningly.

'The time has come to tell the truth, Krishna. Isn't telling the truth, eschewing likes and dislikes, the only dharma, whether it is the mother, wife or son? Is filial love making you mute?' On hearing Narada's question, Krishna looked as if his mind had become clear.

'Samban, right from the day you were born, you were destined to become afflicted with this disease. You have to undergo it. The onset of the disease is upon you. I pronounced it in my rage. That is all. If Narada had not staged this drama, I may have forgotten about it in my love and affection for you. No one can avoid the fruits of destiny. You have somehow angered Narada and have not offered him the respect due to him. He wants you to capitulate to him, so you do that . . . surrender to him.'

'When will this disease leave me? When will my curse leave me? When should I leave this place?'

'Already, we can see the signs of the disease on you. You must leave right away,' Krishna said, unable to continue. He could not look at his son because of his sorrow.

'Samban, leave now. The time is auspicious. Go now. What is sown has to be reaped. You shall live on the riverbanks, unseen by others. Once the disease manifests itself fully, meditate as you focus on me. I'll tell you what to do later on. The one who is strong can bend the sky like a bow. The one who is wise can turn a scrap into a strong pillar. These are testing times for you.' Narada disappeared after saying this.

Samban stood there, stunned and speechless. Sorrow cut his heart like a saw. He was like the worm that had fallen into flames or the fish caught in a hook. Grief rose like a huge wave in his heart and the raging fire inside him could burn not just the city of Dwarka but the entire Yadu clan. But he did not utter a word against his father. He hardened his heart as his mother, Jambavati, did not utter a word either.

'Do your father's bidding.' That was all she said.

He accepted the curse without any resentment as he truly believed it was the fruit of his karma.

Immediately, he forgot his palaces, gold, property, dresses, ornaments, servants, attendants, armies, the captivating Yadava beauties, his glowing wife Lakshmanaa and everything else. The only thing that was in his mind was the curse. Samban's life, which until now was all song and dance and sensual play, had suddenly shattered like a palace in an earthquake. His heart was charred like a tree struck by lightning. He regretted having to give up everything—all his possessions and people. His heart sizzled like a fire pit, but only for a moment and suddenly, his mind was clear.

'As you bid, my father. Your words are my command. Your anger was my curse and so is your love. My being born as your son is also a curse. I have been blessed with curses.'

'Son, take whatever you want with you.'

'I do not want gold, property, elephants, horses or attendants. I shall carry with me only your curse.' He stood with his head bowed before Krishna, who blessed him. Then he went to his three mothers, Rukmini, Satyabama and Jambavati, and prostrated before them. They all wept and embraced him. The Yadu women did not dare to breach their husband's will. *The milk that has come out will not go back into the udders. The butter that has been churned and separated will not re-form into curds, the fallen bloom and the withered fruit will not get back onto the tree. Karma cannot be erased.*

The three mothers then blessed him so that he may get released from the curse.

Samban returned to his palace. He did not meet anyone, not the servants or the Yadu damsels, but only his wife Lakshmanaa. As he explained everything to her, her screams and wails made the palace shake.

'There is no escape from Father's curse. This is fate. This is fate's outcome. It cannot be changed. Bid me farewell.'

She said that she would accompany him but he did not accede to her request.

'Though we are husband and wife, we are not one person. We have been united by circumstance. The curse is on me and not on you, nor will it fall on you. We are two bodies, two souls, two minds, two worlds united only by this conjugal tie.' Samban tried to counsel his wife.

'Have you forgotten how you and I united in conjugal bliss, entwined like *saarai* and *sarpam*, the rat snake and cobra? This is my last desire, let us make love tonight.'

Samban could not turn down her plea. But when they made love that night, only his body engaged in the act. Before the dawn broke and the darkness lightened, Samban took leave of Lakshmanaa with these words:

'The people of the Yadu clan have never criticized their parents. My father has not only cursed me, but

he has also taught me the way of release. I will return
after being released. Wait for me. Do not despair.'

Samban left the city, unseen by anyone.

He then went to the seashore, started staying in
a hut and never stepped out during the day. Now
and then, he could hear the sounds from the city—of
festivities, sports and the cries of young men. On rare
occasions, he saw, from a distance, the Yadu men and
women playing around in a drunken state. Soon after
he started living in solitude, he realized that *life is not
just what the heart desire*s. Memories of his former life
tossed inside him like waves, but he was not grieving
the loss of his royal birth and royal life. His mind was
staggering like a boat in the roaring sea.

Even before a year had passed, his body became
fully covered by the disease. He had become disfigured
and his limbs had started wasting because of the
leprosy. There were sores all over his body and when
his looks changed completely, he went to see Krishna
one day. The people of Dwarka did not recognize him
as Samban. The women who once were drawn towards
his good looks and radiance like moths to a glowing
lamp now shunned him. Not a single soul recognized
him in the streets. Even in the palace, no one recognized
him, not even his wife Lakshmanaa. Only Krishna and
Jambavati knew it was Samban. Jambavati wept and
her tears flowed like a stream on seeing him. Even
Krishna was shocked and he remembered Queen

Gandhari cursing him after the Mahabharata war was over and the Pandavas were being crowned:

> Hey Krishna, O impure one, you destroyed my kingdom. You killed the hundred Kauravas by deceit and cheating. You will weep like I am weeping today, alone as I am, bereft of my sons. You will also weep like this. You will suffer the loss of your child. If I am a *patni*, a faithful wife, this curse will come true.

'Gandhari cursed me and that is why this has befallen you, Samba.'

'Father, I have not come to torment you. I just want to know what I should do next.'

'Meditate on the sage Narada. He alone can tell you what the remedy is. Do not feel sad that Narada had hatched this plot. He did this only to establish dharma and that good may flow as a consequence.'

Samban meditated on Narada and the next moment, found Narada before him. He offered his prayers.

'O great sage, because of my wayward conduct, I failed to offer you my respects. I have received my punishment. Leprosy has spread all over me as cursed by my father. You must bless me by telling me how to get released from this curse.'

Narada was pleased with Samban's reverence.

'O gem of the Vrishni race, your conduct, words, magnanimity and integrity have pleased me. The Sun who shines is the only god that is visible to all. His form is fire. You must pray to him alone. You go at once to the world of the Sun and worship the god of light. The journey will be fraught with misery, but what you suffer will not go to waste. The sins of the father are visited upon their sons and so, you shall have to suffer Gandhari's curse on Krishna. For all the misdeeds committed by Krishna, you as his heir must bear the consequences. It is the curse of a chaste wife, a patni. During the Mahabharata war, Gandhari alone did not commit even one sin. The only sin she was guilty of was muting herself just as she had blindfolded herself.* This curse is that Gandhari's.'

'I bow before your compassion. Where is the world of the Sun? How do I go there?'

'From here, you go toward the shore of the Northern Sea. Once you reach there, you turn north-east and proceed. After a while, you will reach the Chandrabhaga River, a branch of the Prachi River. The Sun God sits there in a resplendent male form. Pray to him and your curse will leave you. If you face hurdles on the way, think of me and pray. I will give you the solution.'

'Great sage, your compassion is my blessing.' Samban bowed before Narada and Krishna and got ready to go to the shrine of the Sun.

---

*This refers to when Gandhari blindfolded herself because her husband was blind and chose not to say anything to correct her sinning son.

'Take with you all the gold that you need, money and servants—as much as you need,' Krishna said.

'Father, forgive me. I have completely forgotten my past life. If I take with me all the things you say, I will not be released from the past. I am not going to attend a banquet. More than the leprosy, it is my earlier life that distresses me and I shun it. My journey is not for pleasure. Whether I gain fame or shame, it all belongs to you. My journey is to release myself from the curse and disease. So, give me your blessings and I will carry that alone with me.'

'Let your wish come true. Let all good happen to you,' Krishna blessed his son who knelt before him. Samban offered his respects to Narada as well.

Samban then left Dwarka. He walked over stones, thorns, hard surfaces, brooks, rivers, mountains, caves and the desert. He walked unmindful of night or day, wind, rain or shine. If he felt hungry, he ate the fruits and roots that he found on his way. When thirsty, he drank the water from the wild streams he passed. Soon after, like the forest dwellers, he had learnt to talk with the streams, hills, rivers, birds, trees, plants and creepers, and would speak whatever was in his mind. In his travels and conversations, he realized the truth that he was alone in this world and that he had no companion but the disease. Immediately, the desire for gold, land and women died like moths in a fire. His mind became clear as the spotless crystal. *The mind builds so many castles in the period between birth and death. Man is the only creature in the world who has base desires, is cunning, deceitful, treacherous, avaricious, and greedy and commits marital infidelity.* When this became clear, he erased all his thoughts of the past. He realized that if he kept remembering his past life, living in the present would become impossible. Gradually, his anger towards Krishna and Narada died down, and he grew more attached to them. He focused on getting released from the curse as he knew this was his fate and he was bound to suffer it. He resolved to prove his innocence, which helped him move on. He saw things he had never seen before and became aware that the mind was a perennially flowing stream. *How can the mind that refuses to be still, be captured? And if it is held back, how long will it stay like that?*

One day, Samban reached a forest at dusk and rested under the shade of a banyan tree. At that moment, he was surrounded by 88,000 species of living creatures—from ants to elephants. None of them harmed him of their own accord. He then thought to himself.

None of these creatures are doing me any harm. Yet, my mind is tossed by anxiety. It is my mind that torments me. If I release myself from my mind's clutches, then there will be no sorrow, no differences—for it is the mind which is the root cause of diseases. The mind pines for the past. First, I must free myself from that. Whether or not

I get released from the curse and the disease, I must
free myself from the mind and its cravings. This is
why I have been cursed. There is no purpose in
finding fault with anyone. I must get freedom from
the mind.

On his journey, Samban came across several streams, ponds, forests, mountains, caves, rivers, beasts and surroundings where there were no human beings. Each of them conveyed to him the same message: 'Samba, you are never going to be cured of the disease. But you will be freed from your mind and its desires. This, you shall know.'

These words were like water sprinkled on parched crops or a lifesaving raft before a drowning man.

One afternoon, he came to a stream. At first, no one wanted to take him on a boat because he was a leper. It is only after he pleaded that they let him climb onto the boat. But none of the passengers spoke to him. He sat in a corner so that he would not cause discomfort to anyone. The boat stopped and he got down. He came to a sea. He walked along the seashore towards the north. He did not know from which point he should turn north. If he went straight northwards, he would reach the Sindhu kingdom ruled by Kuvalayasva's descendants. He remembered the sage Narada telling him that there would be a hermitage there where he could stay. He gained confidence and walked on. It was night, and the crescent moon could be seen. There were some fishermen's huts nearby and he approached them.

'I am coming from Dwarka. I have to go to the Sun temple on the banks of the river Chandrabhaga in the north-east. If you know the way, please tell me.'

'We do not know where it is but we have seen diseased persons like you crossing the river.'

That night, he lay on the river sands at a distance from the huts and fell asleep looking at the moon.

Early the next morning, he crossed the river with the help of fishermen. There, he saw a hermit. He bowed to him and asked about the Sun temple.

'I have heard that there is a temple dedicated to Surya in the Land of the Five Rivers. I have also seen people with skin disease like you, going there and returning freed from the disease. But I do not know how it is cured. If you want to go there, you should not have crossed the river. Go back the way you came.'

Samban offered his respects to him, crossed the river and walked east. He walked in the same direction for seven seasons.* On the first day of the eighth season, he reached the Chandrabhaga River and asked the people there, 'Where is the river Chandrabhaga, the tributary of the Ganges?' Because of his appearance, no one spoke to him except an aged boatman.

'The river you mention is on the other side. Go to the other side and from there, keep walking for

---

* Years.

seven days. On the seventh day, you will come across a stream. If you cross that stream, you will reach that place,' the old man said. Samban bowed to him gratefully. With the boatman's help, he crossed the stream and proceeded as directed by the old man when he reached the other side.

Samban's mind was focused only on the Sun temple. He had lived an aimless life till now—all that he had done was romance women. But now he realized that his body was a nest of worms and he hated himself for what he had done with his nest. Even after losing everything, there was something inside him that glowed like a piece of fire and helped him to go on—it was the sun's glow.

When night came, he lay down in the forest. The fear of wild animals had left him. *Whatever is destined will happen.* Just as one removes the ornaments from their body one by one, all his desires had left him one by one. The difference between night and day had stopped existing for him, as he was now aware that his body was just a bag of air. Differences were only for the desire-filled mind.

He continued his journey the next day after a good night's sleep and reached a stream that evening. After he crossed the stream, he found many huts and asked the people there if this was the shrine of the Sun.

'That's what they say,' a leper replied. All the people around him were lepers and even all the children had the disease.

'Where is the throne of Suryadeva, the king of planets, the *graharaja*?' Samban asked, making the others laugh. One old man among them replied.

'We all came here just like you, upon hearing of this place. But we don't know where exactly it is. There is a temple inside the forest that they say is the *kshetra** of Surya.'

'Have you seen an idol there carved with the image of the king of planets?' Everyone laughed hearing Samban's question.

'There is an idol and we pray there. There is a *rishi*[†] and whenever he sees us, he starts lecturing us. So, we stay away from him. But we do sit where the sunrays fall on us, as advised by him. After that, we leave to beg for alms.'

'Alms?' Samban asked. Everyone laughed and among them, was a young girl called Neelakshi.

'Even if you are a prince, once you come here, you have to beg. Are you the son of a king? You sound like a sage in a forest.' Neelakshi came close to him as she spoke and was almost rubbing against him. She looked repulsive as she was covered in sores and the child at her waist started crying.

'Neelakshi's husband died last night. You can join her from today onwards. You be her partner and her son's father,' the old man told Samban and smiled. The conversation of these people sounded strange to Samban.

---

* The holy location or site.
[†] Sage.

'I can't live with this woman or stay here. You say her husband died just last night. Then how can you speak like this?'

'Rules and laws are there only for those who want to live, not for those who are ready to die. Every day, one man dies here and one man joins us like you did. So, we always live as man and woman, because one must be happy till s/he dies and no one must be alone, for loneliness kills. We are never alone, not even for one night. It may not rain in this forest, but the women never stop having children. Even if you mix honey with the juice of a neem fruit, its bitterness will not change. The broken rice cannot stand too much heat,' one man said.

'What you are doing is wrong. If you fall ill, you must seek the cure, not pursue more diseases,' Samban said.

'You speak like the rishi in the forest and you are also doling out advice like him. At present, I am the only one who is single and without a partner. So, you have to live with me. Here, hold the child.' Neelakshi handed over the child to Samban.

'Neelakshi is right. The number of males here is equal to the number of women and each of us has a partner. Neelakshi alone is single and so are you. We may die tomorrow before it dawns. Why should we not be happy till the last hour? She alone has no joy and neither do you. Embrace her and kiss her tenderly,' was the advice of an old man in the group.

'I will never do something so crass and vile. I have given up sensual love long ago and will not do this improper act. How can you be sure that we will die? We did not come here to die. Didn't you all come here with the hope that you will be cured? That thought is our hope, it is our life. If we lose that, we are just corpses.'

'Who are you to advise us?' The crowd charged towards Samban but Neelakshi intervened. She shouted at the crowd and told them to listen to Samban. The crowd calmed down.

'Don't forget why you came here. Don't abandon hope. Nurture the desire to get cured and to return to your home. Your desire or your aim does not cause harm or misery to others. Our future lies in our hope. Let us not be despicable creatures' Samban said.

'He speaks like a hermit or like a king's son,' the people muttered as they returned to their huts.

Neelakshi and Samban remained outside. She rubbed against him, hugged him, kissed him and lured him in many ways to draw him into her hut but he was unmoved. She then shared some of the food she had got as alms, which he ate.

'You speak strangely. I will not couple with you. I will always be your companion, your brother. I will be like the lamp's wick, lighting up your life,' Samban said and spent the night outside Neelakshi's hut. Before the day broke, he started to walk east. On his way, he saw a thousand lovely blooms and felt like spending the rest of his life there—he could even smell the fragrance of the magizham flower. He asked himself how he would bow to Aditya, the Sun when he saw him, how he would offer his prayers and how he would be freed from his curse. He prayed with all his heart, circumambulated thrice and walked towards the stream. The sun rose then in the eastern sky like a ball of kumkum, a sphere of fire, and he folded his palms in respect.

He saw a sage worshipping Adhisakthiswara and approached him and prostrated himself before him.

'Respected sage, I have come here stricken with leprosy because of a curse.' The sage asked him to follow him to his hermitage. He then told him to sit in the south-east, looking at the sun and that he would speak to him after his prayers. The sage went to do his puja while Samban sat in the sun as bidden by the sage. He started meditating on the Sun god. His eyes were closed, his body was motionless but his mind was not silent.

'Suryadeva, release me from this curse. I have detached myself from gold, wealth and women. Release me from my mind too.'

Lost in meditation, he opened his eyes only when he heard the sage's voice.

'Have these fruits after you have prayed to the king of planets,' the sage said. Samban bowed to him and took the fruits from him.

'Tell me your story,' the sage asked Samban, sitting in front of him.

'What story can a clay pot, a shell, have, swami? This is a body that will be reduced to a fistful of ashes, a sack filled with desires.' The sage looked at him curiously as he realized that Samban was a man of wisdom, not like the others, and that he knew of the eight karmas.

'Why have you come here?'

'Liberation. To be released from the curse.'

'Curse?'

'Yes, swami.'

'Who told you about this place?'

'The sage Narada.'

'Narada? Have you seen him? Have you seen Narada who can travel across space and time? I can't believe it. Then you are indeed fortunate. Who are you?'

'Swami, show me your compassion, please do not get angry. I will tell you who I am at the right time.'

'As you wish.'

'In the morning, you folded your palms before the Sun god, but you did not perform puja. Why?'

'I have the right to study the Vedas, but not to do puja. I am a Brahmin belonging to *Devaloka*.* I draw the image of the sun on the ground with vermilion paint and offer my salutations. I do not know who made this Sun temple. This is the place of origin and the place of setting for the king of planets. When he

---

* The abode of gods in Hindu mythology.

radiates on one side of this earth, his last rays have special powers. They are capable of curing many skin diseases. That is why I came here. Since then, I have been worshipping the setting Surya. My skin disease has gradually disappeared.'

'Is this the only such place?'

'The sun first appears in this country from behind the Udayachala hill. Since he rises in the north-east corner he is called "Konaditya" or Aditya in the corner. It is here in the south-west that he sets. The place where he sits at noon is to the south of Yamuna and is near Dwarka. In that form, he is called "Kaalapriya".* To be cured of leprosy, the sun's rays must fall on the body at all three times—dawn, noon and dusk.'

'How is it possible to go to all three places in the same day?'

'We must divide the year into three periods and go to that appropriate place at that particular time. I too did the same. The king of planets has twelve names— Aditya, Savita, Surya, Mitra, Arka, Prabhakara, Marthanda, Bhaskara, Bhanu, Chitrabhanu, Ravi and Divakara. He bears these twelve names and is seated in twelve places during the twelve months. If you go to those places during the respective months and bathe in the holy streams nearby, you will be cured.'

'Which are these holy places?'

---

*The sun has twelve *kaala* or phases. This probably means 'dear to the phases'.

'Pushkara, Naimisha Kurukshetra, Pruthoodaka, Ganga, Saraswathi, Sindhu, Chandrabhaga, Payaswini, Yamuna, Tamra and Kshipra. It will take six seasons to go to all these places. Can you do it?'

'With your blessings and grace, I can do it, swami.'

'On *valarpirai sapthami,* the seventh day of the waxing moon in every month, the sun's rays have special potency. On that day, you must fast and worship him.'

'What should I do next?' Samban asked with humility.

'You visit the twelve sites and come back. I will tell you then.'

'I want to take all the others with the disease along with me.'

'They never listen to anyone, nor do they respect anyone. They are the lowest of the low. Can you make them whole, the pots that are broken?'

'With your grace, swami, it can be done.'

The sage was pleased.

'My fullest blessings are with you always. Farewell.' Samban bowed to him and went to the huts of the lepers. They surrounded him and started to mock him.

'The sage must have poured his advice on you.'

This treatment saddened him.

'Don't speak disrespectfully of the rishi. He is greater than all of us. Learn to worship him. He is a *mahapurusha*.'* No one paid heed to his words and made fun of both the sage and Samban. Then, Neelakshi came with a bowl in hand after her daily routine of begging for alms.

'Did your bowl get filled up?' Samban asked her.

'No.'

'It will never get filled up. That is the curse of the begging bowl.'

'You are forever talking of the curse. What I have got is sufficient. Come, I will share it with you. Eat.'

'Give me, I'll eat. After tonight, I am going on a journey. Come with me.'

'What journey? Why are you calling me? Instead of remaining here till you die, why do you want to roam around?' She came close to him and her body touched his.

'It is not enough to quench the fire in our bellies. We must cool the fire raging in our hearts. I am a blemish on the human race. I will not hurt you. I will not commit base acts with you. Please do not provoke me to commit sinful deeds. My family would never commit the five deadly sins, for that would bring ill repute. I was not born into a wicked family. Dasaratha died because he listened to Kaikeyi. Rama suffered as he chased the deer as bidden by Sita. Ravana, along with his kith and kin, died as he listened to Surpanaka. So, obeying a woman is not righteous. I

---
* An illustrious and noble person.

may unite with a demon but not a woman. Forget all this and sleep—that is the only medicine for you. Once you realize that this body is a nest of worms, you will know lust is nothing. Why did you come to this place?'

'To get cured of leprosy.'

'Has it gone?'

'No.'

'What effort have you taken to achieve it?'

'Nothing.'

'That is your mistake. If you do nothing, how will it go? I am going on a pilgrimage with that objective in mind. I am a leper just like you but I have hope. So, I am going to visit twelve holy places, bathe in twelve holy rivers and pray to Surya to get cured.'

'None of us will go with you. He is a liar. A dangerous trickster. He is trying to ruin us with his magic,' the rabble shouted but Neelakshi controlled them.

'Don't preach to us. Tell us what those places are,' she asked him.

'What is left for you in this life?'

'Death.'

'Then why didn't you die in your own place? Why did you come here?'

'We had hope then, but not any more.'

'That is the problem. Losing hope is the trouble. The only thing left with us is hope. It is because you lost hope that you became like this. Will anyone who goes to bathe, smear themselves with muck? You need to firmly believe that we will become cured and then we will be,' Samban promised them. He told them about the disease, its cure, the Surya temples, the holy sites, the holy rivers and so on.

'How do you know all this?'

'The hermit in the forest told me. The sage Narada also told me.'

'Narada told you?' the crowd asked.

'Yes.' He told them all that Narada had said without revealing his own identity. Then at the end, he asked, 'Who will come with me in the morning? The path we take is that of the Siddhas, the sages, the ascetics and Siva. So, we will always have the grace of God.'

'I'll come with you,' Neelakshi said. She then spoke with the others and won them over. At night, they all sat under the moonlight and asked Samban for details about the holy rivers and listened to him all night. Before the dawn broke and the darkness dispersed, they bathed in the river, gathered before the sage and fell at his feet. The sage was surprised.

'Fare you well. You won't fail in your venture. You will succeed in achieving your objective. And when you achieve success, you attain enlightenment. You will leave this world and reach heaven. God resides not in benighted minds. If you follow the austerities as ordained on seven sapthamis, the disease will disappear.'

Samban was followed by seventy others on his journey.

They went to all the twelve places and bathed in the twelve rivers. Twelve seasons had gone by when they returned to the shrine of the setting sun near Chandrabhaga River. There were only fifteen persons left, including Samban, as many had died during the journey due to ill-health and some had stayed back, being unable to continue. The women who lost their husbands and children abused Samban with cruel words—it was Neelakshi who pacified all of them.

Even before twelve seasons had passed, there was an improvement in their health. The numbness was going away and their sensations were slowly getting restored. The hair on their head and brows stopped falling, and beards and moustaches began to grow on the men's faces. The wasting of their bodies had stopped.

When they were crossing the river Sindhu, Samban found a wooden statue that resembled the idol of the Sun god. He went to the sage with the statue and offered his prayers with all humility. The sage was mightily pleased and bestowed his blessings on Samban and the others.

'Samba, install this wooden idol here. It is made of the karpaka tree, which is from Devaloka. Now you must get prepared for another stupendous task. Some time ago, I told you I did not have the right to perform puja, remember? There are Brahmins on the island of

Saka who have the right to do it and you must bring them to Bharatavarsha. They have calculated and ascertained which puja is to be done at which time for curing leprosy, and also know the medical treatment for the disease. Some of them used to live here, but they went back because they were not given the due respect. Going to Saka is arduous, like a mouse burrowing its way through a mountain. First, you go to Antariksha, then the Devaloka, Ilavrtavarsha and beyond that, the Sakadwipa or the Saka Island. Go there and bring the qualified Brahmins. But before that, you install this wooden statue.'

'As you wish.'

'First, you must bring the people of the Viswakarma clan to construct the temple for this statue. They are in the region which is to the south-west from here. To bring them here and maintain them, you need a lot of wealth. I am a mendicant and you are a leper. What can we do?' The sage was filled with worry.

'Swami, I shall arrange for the wealth.'

'How can you do it?' the sage asked in surprise. Samban narrated his story to him.

'Has the son of that Krishna, who waged the Mahabharata war single-handedly, been afflicted by this disease? Are you the son of Krishna whom the world worships?'

'Swami, my past life does not attract me. I have given it up like the snake sloughs its skin. This physical frame is not a frame of fame, it is an abode of worms.

The sword cannot cure the disease. Anyway, this disease and the curse are not my priority now. My goal is to install this idol and build a temple, and for that, I have to bring the Brahmins from Saka. Bless me so that I achieve my goal. I will leave for Dwarka right away.'

'Samba, there is much to learn from you. You have very noble qualities. In a few days, it will be the seventh day of the waxing moon. Install the idol of Suryadeva on that day and leave the next day. Your task will be successful and you will live forever. Your fame will spread in the fourteen worlds. Make this place a holy site.'

Samban bowed to the sage. The people with him were stunned to hear his story. They could not believe that he was the son of Krishna and wanted to fall at his feet, but he stopped them.

'I am not Krishna's son now. I am a leper and one of you. My life will end in your midst. You alone are my family.' He embraced each one of them. The afflicted ones shed tears.

'We must start making arrangements to install the idol. The day after the installation, I must go to Dwarka. I can do all this only with your assistance.'

'We will follow your orders implicitly,' they said in one voice. With Neelakshi following him like a shadow, Samban met the newly arrived persons with the disease before he went to sleep.

The idol was installed and Neelakshi told Samban to leave for Dwarka the next day.

'Samba, we must build the Sun temple. Go to Dwarka at once,' she said, but her eyes were wet. Ever since she knew who Samban was, she had maintained a distance from him and Samban recognized her reserve.

'Neelakshi, you are the inspiration for my deeds. Without you, nothing would have been achieved. You are like my guiding light. It is because of the glow from you that I could visit the twelve holy sites and bathe in those rivers. Next to the Sun god, I owe my respect to you.' Neelakshi broke down when she heard Samban's words.

'I approached you in lust in a most unacceptable way. I desired you. That was my body's failing. You are the reason why I am alive today. You opened my eyes. It is through you that I see the world now. I am a truly fortunate woman. It was you who showed me the difference between the mind and the body. This body is a hollow vessel, a mud pot. You are the root that holds me to this earth. You are my way. Every day, I mentally pray to you, as the guru of my clan, my *kulaguru*.'

'Neelakshi, you are a rare blossom in the forest. You alone are my mentor and guide. Your love, compassion and large-heartedness lead me. Neelakshi, my friend, who shows compassion like a mother. You and the others please bless me to go on this voyage.' He arranged for a horse, took their leave and sped like the wind to Dwarka.

Samban reached Dwarka in a month. Krishna was boundlessly happy to see him, and Jambavati and the other mothers shed tears of joy and welcomed him with warm embraces. The palace vibrated with happiness, but just for a moment because Samban told them that he was there only for a night. It was like molten hot lead poured down their ears. All of them wept and tried to change his mind, but he was steadfast in his resolve and could not be moved. He explained the object of his voyage and calmed them all, but comforting Lakshmanaa was as difficult as crossing an ocean. He stayed that night and left Dwarka early the next morning, taking with him abundant wealth.

Samban's chariot went as fast as a hurricane and soon, he met the people of the Viswakarma clan. Once he told them what his plans were, he gave them all the wealth they needed and came back with them to the site after a month. There, he made arrangements to build the Sun temple and with Neelakshi's help, he finished the task in seven months. On the first day of the eighth month, he recommenced his journey and all the others who were stricken with the disease bade him farewell.

He crossed the land stretch of the Five Rivers and reached the foothills of the Himalayas after a month. From there, he proceeded to Antariksha. As he approached the Antariksha, he started sighting the Gandharvas, the demigods. They were all very good-looking and rode on horses and mountain goats. Antariksha was situated amidst small mountains and Samban crossed the river there with the help of a boat.

He then asked how he should go to Ilatavarsha and travelled towards the north-west. By the time he reached Sakadwipa, ten months had gone by. The residents of Saka Island looked like gods. When he met the elders of the Magar community who lived there, he offered them fruits, flowers, darbha grass and tirumanjana water—all the ritualistic offerings of respect. He then told them what he had come for.

'Your acts and deeds fill us with trust. We have heard of Krishna. My people will come there. But will they be duly respected?' a Magar elder asked Samban.

'O priests who recite the Vedas! I will offer expensive clothes and ornaments and give rich perfumes like *kasturi*.* I will make the appropriate gifts and payments. I will give lands, milch cows and cattle, and everything you want like gold and other wealth. You will have no cause to complain. Eighteen families should come with me and the puja must be done at the Sun temple built by me. Our country is ridden with leprosy, you must also erase it completely. This is my plea.'

The Magars trusted Samban and so, eighteen families prepared to go to Bharatavarsha with him. They climbed onto chariots driven by mules, horses and mountain goats and set out.

When Samban returned to the site of the Sun temple with the Magars, he was happy to see that the

---

* Musk.

Sun temple which was being constructed in the form of a chariot was halfway complete. The Magars saw that Samban had not misled them and praised him. The foundation was laid for building a *homasalai*, a hall for the performance of *homas*, the sacrificial rites. During the journey, the Magars had administered treatment to Samban for his disease and the signs of the cure were clearly visible.

On seeing Samban's improvement, the others were overjoyed. They marvelled at it and prayed to the Magars that they also be cured.

He then left behind six Magar families in that place and took the other Magars along with a few of the Viswakarmas and went to Mathura on the southern banks of Yamuna and established a homasalai there. He requested the Viswakarma people to build a Sun temple and made six Magar families remain there. Then he took the remaining Magars and Viswakarmas and went to Utra. There, he built a homasalai where the Chandrabhaga River meets the sea. He requested the Viswakarmas to build a temple for the Sun god and asked the remaining six Magar families to stay there. Both the Magars and the Viswakarmas applauded his deed and dedicated themselves to building the temple. Samban took leave of all of them and set off to return to the site of the Sun god.

A year had gone by when he returned and a small town had come up. He was struck with wonder as the citizens of the town had named it 'Sambapur'. The leprosy-afflicted were restored to health by the Magar Brahmins' treatment and new patients had joined them. Pujas were performed at the Suryadeva temple thrice a day, in the morning, noon and evening. Samban's heart was filled with joy upon seeing everything.

'The Vedic norms must be adhered to. Dharma will flourish only if there is righteousness and right conduct,' he told the Magars and then went to see the sage in the forest.

He spent four months each at three holy places on the eastern shore—Kaalapriya, Kaalanathala and Konavallabathala—as bidden by the sage and one year went by. With his old companions, he supervised the activities in the three temples. As he approached each of the temples, they appeared like the devas' world. On the outside of the temple, there were statues of devas, yakshas, gandharvas and apsaras. The temple was constructed like a huge chariot and there were four entrances. The guardians of the entrances were Pingala, Dandanayaka, Rajna, Stosha, Kalmasa, Pakshi, Vyoma and Nagnadindi. The Adityas, Vasus, Maruts and Aswinis were in their respective places as well. In twelve years, all three temples were fully constructed.

One day, when Samban said he was going to Konarka and staying there to worship Konaditya, Neelakshi expressed what was on her mind.

'I am not made of stone. I am a human being. You are my greatest friend, my *mahamaitra*, you are like my life. So, you must come here at least once a year. That is my final wish.'

'Neelakshi, I have not forgotten our first meeting or that night. You fed me that day and I will never forget that either. If you had not been there, nothing could have been accomplished. You were the one who gave me hope that day. So, you are the source of my strength, my *adhimulasakthi*. You stood tall because of your wisdom and intelligence, which made the patients comply with your words. All of you toiled to raise these three temples. You live by your deeds. That is why you became my sister, Neelakshi.'

Neelakshi fell at Samban's feet with tears in her eyes.

'Samba, if you had not come here, I would have become dust long ago. I would not have seen the temples of Suryadeva and the twelve holy sites. I would not have bathed in the twelve holy rivers. Now I am restored to my original condition, but that is not important. Only you are. It was you who revealed Suryadeva to me. You are my guiding spirit. From now on, this forest will be called *Mitravanam*.'*

Samban was filled with emotion and tears flowed from his eyes. He hugged her tight and promised, 'My maitreyi, my dear friend, a maitreya of the forest will not break the word he gives to his maitreyi. This Mitravanam is a brother's gift to his sister. I will visit you every year.'

---

*Forest of friendship.

'This word is enough. This is my ornament, my treasure,' Neelakshi said.

As Samban took leave of everyone, Narada appeared before him and Samban welcomed him with due reverence.

'Samba, your old form is restored. Your curse has been lifted. Leave at once to Dwarka. You are no longer accursed,' Narada announced.

'Most respected one, I do not intend to return to Dwarka ever.'

'Why? Your people are waiting for you.'

'I have understood the meaning of life. I have realized what the mind is. The life I wish for is not in Dwarka, it is here in this Mitravanam. Even if I am given mountains of gems of all kinds, I will not go back. I plan to spend the rest of my life worshipping Suryadeva. I do not desire gold or land. Those desires died long ago. I have severed the old memories. Bless me, O great sage. On my way to the place of the Sun god, I had to stay in burial grounds where demons, spirits and wicked venomous creatures play about. I have slept in the densest of forests and the most barren fields. I have spent many nights just looking at the stars and moon. It was then that I realized that this life is as transient as a lamp in a hurricane. Human life is the smallest of trifles. I had a father and a mother. I had elephants, armies, troops, palaces and boundless wealth. But when I came here, I came alone, the solitary me. The disease alone accompanied me. When I go to the cremation ground, I will go alone. This was the lesson taught to me during those nights. I cherish the memory of those nights like a treasure. I do not need any other wealth. This man, this woman is a glob of flesh. This, too, I have learnt.'

Narada was filled with joy as though he had drunk the divine nectar, the *devamritham*.

'Samba, you have erected three temples to Suryadeva, a task no one else has done. So, your name will remain eternal in all the worlds forever. Even the gods will acclaim you. Come, let us worship Suryadeva together.' Narada took him along into the temple.

'O graharaja, king of planets, who is worshipped by all sentient beings, all the gods and all the Vedas, please accept my puja,' Narada prayed to the sun.

'From today, the king of planets will be called Sambadithyan. That is the name by which he will be worshipped,' Narada declared.

Samba, who had not shed a tear when he was cursed, cried now. Narada embraced him and asked him what he intended to do next.

'I am going to the riverbank. If any new lepers have arrived, I will bring them here and make them worship Suryadeva.'

He bowed to Narada and walked towards the riverbank.

Scan QR code to access the
Penguin Random House India website